The M

by

Thomas Neviaser

The Mystery of Flight 2222 - Text copyright
© Thomas Neviaser 2018

Editing and Cover Art by Emmy Ellis @
studioenp.com © 2018

All Rights Reserved

The Mystery of Flight 2222 is a work of fiction. All characters, places, and events are from the author's imagination. Any resemblance to persons, living or dead, events or places is purely coincidental.

The author respectfully recognizes the use of any and all trademarks.

With the exception of quotes used in reviews, this book may not be reproduced or used in whole or in part by any means existing without written permission from the author.

Warning: The unauthorized reproduction or distribution of this copyrighted work is illegal. No part of this book may be scanned, uploaded, or distributed via the Internet or any other means, electronic or print, without the author's written permission.

Prologue

The Law of Karma
Nothing happens by chance or outside Universal Laws.
Every action has a reaction and consequence, and we reap what we have sown.

In other words, what goes around comes around!

Chapter One

Kate entered the bedroom. *He couldn't find a sink in his own bathroom.*

Frank Mason, her athletic, six-foot-two husband of nine years—a handsome man with relatively sharp features to his full-shaven face, short brown hair, and steel-gray eyes—was late for his flight and frantically searching the closet for his dress shoes. She had often been told he resembled Rod Serling of the famous television show, *Twilight Zone.* God, she'd never get over how he forgot where he'd put things.

Without a word, Kate reached behind an old overcoat in the closet, and, voila, there were his shoes.

She held the shoes up and turned to Frank, raising her eyebrows. If he lost it, Kate always found it. She smiled, shook her head, and while her husband continued packing, she left the room. She would know by the increasing sound of footsteps and cussing if he needed her to reappear.

What would he do without me? He's such a take-charge type of guy at work.

As Kate waited for him to find everything he needed, she was torn between wanting him to be successful in this venture and his absence for possible weeks away while she was pregnant. It was her first pregnancy, and she really needed him there for support and love during this scary nine months that would change their lives forever. She hated his trips with a passion. As with every new mother-to-be, worries about what may happen always popped into her head and made her fearful.

Frank's job—the thing that took him away from her—was a stock analyst for a very distinguished corporation. His twelve years of steady, positive input had been rewarded continuously by the board with substantial salary raises as well as intermittent, sizable bonuses.

Life was good! His traveling was one small bone of contention at times, but even though she hated being apart from him, Kate understood that his rise in the company would depend on his ability to travel. All of this scurrying here and there would end someday.

She sighed. This trip to Buenos Aires hadn't been in the cards. It had been a spur-of-the-moment decision by the upper echelon of the company. He had been hand-picked for his tenure and excellent people-management skills. In Argentina, there was a fledgling company with a hot-shot CEO, and Frank's bosses thought it would be a spectacular chance for his corporation to get in on the bottom tier financially before it became well-known.

With Frank's flight leaving at eight that night and having to get there two hours early, Kate planned a sumptuous dinner for Frank at five, a bit earlier than usual. She needed to have that special time with her man, and she didn't want him leaving on an empty stomach. She worked feverishly to make it outstanding, giving her something to do to take her mind off her worries.

Kate showed an inexplicable expression of uneasiness while they sat for dinner, causing Frank to pick up his plate and glass of wine and move to the seat closest to her. Kate smiled, grasped his hand, and leaned over and kissed him on the cheek.

"Wow, soft shell crabs? What an exquisite dinner! Man, I haven't had these forever," Frank exclaimed, waving his hands above his shoulders as if he had just scored a touchdown.

"Brenda told me about this guy who comes up from the coast with these frozen every Friday and Saturday, so I bought some. Cheap, I think," Kate replied.

"How much?" Frank asked.

"Two for seven bucks."

"Wow, that's a bargain. Get some more so I can have them when I get back," he said.

After dinner, they both huddled around the sink, Kate scrubbing off the plates and Frank putting them in the dishwasher. As he closed the door to the washer, he said, "Mighty fine dining here tonight. I think that's worth a twenty percent tip."

Kate held out her hand in response, waiting for his extremely extravagant tip. Then she laughed and replied, "Get your butt up there and be sure you didn't leave anything like your ticket, glasses, and..."

Frank had already started upstairs to check if he indeed did overlook anything, so she didn't get a chance to list all the things that he had forgotten in the past. Without a doubt, an object would slip his mind, for sure, so he always checked. Despite his ritual, Frank would fail to remember something important, so it became a game for them as to which one found his last item.

"Kate! Have you seen my nail clippers?"

"Geez, Frank, get one at the airport," she said with a snide soft giggle as she stood by the stairs below.

Kate knew he'd given up hunting for the clippers and felt confident he did not leave anything else behind, for he appeared at the top of the stairs and proceeded to descend in a cocky posture to where she was waiting with his cellphone in her hands.

"Dang it and hang it, I really thought I had you this time," he said.

Kate dangled the phone above a little purple canvas bag in which she had placed one of Frank's favorite snacks so he did not have to stand in line to buy some munchies at the airport. Frank had confided in her that he had made a habit of never looking into this gift bag straight away, always hoping to be surprised by her ingenuity later on.

Kate watched while he took the phone, put it in his inside coat pocket, and placed the purple bag in one of the pockets of the cargo travel pants he always wore on flights. He then pulled his travel-weary bag, applying pressure to the inside of the handle to compensate for the one wobbly wheel on the outside. She shook her head as her knight approached the front door on his way to his mighty steed, the family SUV.

"Uh, you forget something, Frank?" she asked.

"As if there would be a day I wouldn't forget, but this time I didn't forget it. I left my briefcase in the car. So there, fancy pants. I win! Ha!"

"Oh my, such a wonderful man, but not very thoughtful." She laughed, pointing to her pursed lips.

"Christ! I lost again. Damn, I was going to come back and smack those luscious lips. You knew that, right?"

"Sure. I knew that, right?" Kate replied, mimicking the question he'd just asked while trying her best to look sexy.

"Yeah, you caught me again," he said sheepishly.

The wooden stairs to the porch creaked as he ascended to his damsel. Their arms entwined, and a long kiss ensued. Their heads separated, and they stood face to face looking into each other's eyes. Kate's welled up, and tears began flowing. It always happened when he finished kissing her goodbye. She always knew he felt somewhat guilty every time he left, knowing she would be alone for a week, sometimes weeks at a time. He slid his hand down to her expanded belly and patted it, caressed it, and leaned down and spoke to her abdomen.

"And I'll be back to love you, too, sweet cakes!" As he rose up, she hoped her face was magically illuminated with a glow of everlasting love.

"It's not as if I'll be on a raft for fifty-two days, mi amor. Besides, how the hell can I ever forget that face?" he whispered in her ear. "I'll get things done as fast as possible, love."

How can I get through this trip without him?

She then laughed and shrugged, rotated to her left, and jiggled her rear. Frank laughed, too, and carefully backed down the steps, their hands slipping from their outstretched arms, and he then turned toward the car. He got in, closed the door, and started the car as Kate anxiously waited. He looked up, saw her, opened the door, and ran up the stairs for one more embrace and another long kiss. Once again, he backed down the stairs, slowly holding her hand again until it slid out.

As he drove out of sight, he continued waving out the window as he rounded the corner well out of Kate's sight. She had told him she always continued to wave even though she realized he couldn't see her, too. They both knew, in their hearts, the other was still waving, and each did not want to stop for fear the other would.

~~ ~~ ~~

Frank drove the SUV into the parking garage at the JFK Airport, being sure to be as close to the exit to the terminal as possible so he didn't have far to walk when he got back. The excitement of leaving was enough to give him energy to drag his luggage, his carry-on, and briefcase with his computer. He placed the parking ticket in his briefcase and marched toward the terminal for the Air USA Flight 2222. He had chosen an economy seat just to show the partners that he was frugal and not a spendthrift. This irked him tremendously, since his legs were long and really cramped in the 'cheap seats.' Once he had his boarding passes, he kept his driver's license in his hand to be sure he would be able to show it to the TSA's attendees along with his boarding passes. He just hated 'disrobing' and placing everything in his pocket into one or two of those gray baskets, pulling his computer out of his briefcase, and taking his shoes and belt off. Once it was his turn to go through the body scanner, he threw up his arms in the proper position and was notified that he had something in his pocket and had to remove it. He patted his trousers but didn't feel anything. He was frisked with a wand first, and the buzzer went off over the pocket containing Kate's purple bag.

"Dang, I forgot, Officer. I'm sorry."

He gave the bag to the agent, and as it was opened, there were his nail clippers. The agent replaced them, gave the bag back, and signaled for him to pick up the rest of his gear.

"Thank you, sir," he said as he started to redress himself. He felt like a fool not remembering the bag was stashed away in the lower pocket of his cargo pants, but he accepted his mistake and trudged off to Gate 47. Once there, he scanned the waiting area for a seat, hopefully with an empty one next to it, to place his carry-ons. He then sat and tried to relax.

Relaxing was not easy for him, though. His mind was continuously mulling over everything: his ticket, keys, driver's license, proper paperwork for the meetings, and telephone numbers needed to call for information in Argentina. Over and over, he ran these types of things through his brain to be sure he had everything. After all, he knew he easily forgot things, and Kate certainly could vouch for this.

Helen Hampton left the shop early. Although she was worried, her employees knew that this trip was one she had to make. Her mother-in-law's illness had hung over her marriage for so long that her husband, Ricardo, had become disillusioned with her. Her mean remarks about Rick's mother pretending to be sick to get his attention were cute in the beginning, but as the disease started to consume her mother-in-law's body, those comments had been very much out of line. Possibly because she was so involved in her own flower business, she just never saw Maria slowly wasting away.

Helen had met Ricardo, a stylist, in a hair salon. She was impressed with his ability to cut and style hair to each woman's anatomical features and their personality. The dashing way about him, his laughter, and mannerisms all captivated her, and she fell in love. She knew Ricardo felt the same way, but it took a year of Helen being his customer before he finally understood what love was.

Their marriage started with a visit to Argentina to meet his family. Everyone there seemed to be impressed with Helen, and she felt at home. Life was hectic with Helen starting her own business and

Ricardo trying to expand his. They had no children. Neither wanted any, and it was never discussed, just understood. Both felt children would be a drag on their successes, and they were probably correct in thinking so. Helen was an only child, and being the only one, she felt she was a princess. She always thought that if she had a sibling, she might have resented her or him, and that resentment may well have destroyed their family.

After five years, Maria got sick and wasn't able to get good care in Argentina. The family there was not wealthy enough for what care was available, either. Helen encouraged Ricardo to apply for a special visa and to get Maria to the United States and get the proper care, and after several years of misdiagnoses, they found out that she had a debilitating disease that was causing her muscular wasting. Helen was not a patient woman. For years, the doctors didn't know the reason for Maria's symptoms, and Helen eventually came to her own conclusion that Maria was making it all up to keep her son close and away from her. It began as a game to Helen. Maria would say one thing, and Helen would rebut her with some funny or whimsical remark, but as time passed, she became more angry at Maria. Her barbs were increasingly caustic and sometimes downright mean. Helen was sure that Maria was trying to break up her marriage and take Ricardo from her. That was when she opted to start her own business, to get away from Maria during the day and only have to see her late in the evenings.

She had been so consumed by being successful with the floral business that her marriage suffered, and, being headstrong and a control freak, she spent her waking hours fighting for every bit of business she could. This stress caused her to consider her mother-in-law a verbal punching bag when she was home with Rick. He loved his mother with all his heart and began to pull away from Helen in silent disgust. Not until Maria was finally diagnosed with a rare disease was it obvious she had not been pretending to be sick. Helen finally realized her torturing of Rick and Maria with snide comments had been terribly mean and divisive, but Rick could no longer abide by her actions and words. Rick took his mother home to Argentina and stayed there.

Rick and Helen had been divorced for two years. The news of Maria's passing was not unexpected, but still, Helen was surprised. Why, she did not understand. When she finally faced her emotions, she knew she had to go to the funeral whether or not Rick and the rest of his family liked it. She had to pay her respects, and, at least in her mind, make amends. Was it enough? For them, probably not, but for her, she hoped yes. She was so overcome by guilt at times, she couldn't even get it together enough to conduct the daily activities of the business. Ambivalence was not just a word now. It was an overwhelming feeling pulling her apart for hours at a time. Her guilt was intense, totally engrossing her daily. She just had to do something, and this trip seemed to be the answer—at least, in her mind.

Folding every blouse and skirt meticulously, she placed each item of clothing neatly in her suitcase, the larger clothes on the bottom and the smaller ones packed snugly on top. Her final addition was a plain, newly ironed black dress. She held it up in front of her, walked to the full-length mirror in her bathroom, and gazed at it for a while, wondering if she was making the correct decision. She folded it and laid it on top of the rest of the garments. She stared at it as if it would give her some answer to her conundrum. Then, she touched it as if to goad it into giving her some response. She turned to place the last few makeup items in the bag, and, with one last swipe, she smoothed out the black dress slowly and deliberately.

Visions of her in that dress appearing at the funeral and the subsequent home visits for family and friends popped in and out of her head, some frighteningly offensive and others of being ostracized completely. She had to have some kind of closure whether or not the rest of the family wanted to have anything to do with her. She had decided not to inform them she was coming but often thought she should at least tell them of her arrival. Then again, she thought she was so disliked, the family would change plans just to avoid her. Helen felt uneasy with this awful dilemma. She finally stuck with the surprise visit and hoped for the best.

Helen turned to the bathroom mirror and

studiously examined herself; her pudgy face, overly pink cheeks, brunette hair in ringlets on one side opposed to the stringy broken ends on the other. She wondered how anyone would ever be attracted to her and how she'd ruined her marriage with Rick.

Her psyche had been severely damaged, and it was all her fault. She should have known better, but for some reason, she had been so sure Maria had been faking it.

How could I have been so damn dumb? All the signs were there. I never saw them. How blind can one be and be able to see? On the other hand, Rick never saw my side of it. If he had, he would have noticed Maria was often mean-spirited.

She definitely missed Rick's ability to style her hair. None of the salons she used now could match it. She ran her fingers through the forest of stringy hair as she stood gazing into the mirror that was reflecting a very disparaging image of the woman Rick had fallen in love with. She stood sideways, pushed out her stomach, and then sucked it in.

"Godzilla, the female monster, right here, ladies and gentlemen." She turned away from the mirror, switched the light off, and exited the bathroom.

Snapping the leather lid and fastening two belts around her bag, she ran her hand gently over the suitcase and sat by it on the edge of the bed for a few minutes. Her mind was blank. She wasn't thinking of anything, just sitting there. She stood and walked into the kitchen where she filled her cup with instant decaffeinated coffee and hot water. Fat-free milk was the only addition to her old standby beverage. She'd become hooked on this milk when she'd tried to diet many times unsuccessfully. Sure, it was like drinking white acrid water, but changing back to any milk with fat made her uneasy.

The clock on the wall showed three-thirty in the afternoon. She had plenty of time to make it to the airport. There was no rush, but she felt strangely hurried. After all, she was

flying to Argentina where she did not speak the language, and the only people she knew were her ex-husband and his family, a group who did not consider her a relative much less a friend. She could only imagine the reception she would encounter. She had bought an English to Spanish guide book, tried to read it for the last couple of weeks so she could communicate with the people there but didn't really have her heart in it.

A phone ringing brought her to her senses.

"Hello? Oh, yes, I'm okay, Mel. Please, I'll be fine. I appreciate all of your concerns. Tell the rest goodbye, hear?"

She had done all her homework. She'd made sure Mel, her manager, knew exactly how she wanted the business run. Mel was short for Melanie, who insisted Helen call her such after she was promoted from a floral designer to manager. Helen thought it was because it sounded more like a man's name and, therefore, gave her more confidence to do the job and keep tabs on the employees. It also may have been because Mel's voice was lower than most women's, and Mel would have been construed as a male over the phone, giving her an advantage, especially if talking to a man, but she'd never asked Mel why.

She had spent the last week going over and over the duties Mel was expected to perform: opening and closing the store, watching the cash register like a hawk, attending to the complaints of specific customers and some employees whom she listed on a piece of paper and slid under the drawer inside the cash register. Mel was more than capable doing all of this and more, but Helen had to get her two cents in again and again. Mel accepted her overbearing quirks. Helen soon felt secure leaving with Mel on watch for her.

At five, she cooked her dinner, poured a glass of red wine, and sat pondering her next days away from home. Her mind raced here and there, creating scenarios that she could meet head-on agreeably and would seem truly repentant and not obnoxious. She so desperately wanted everyone to know she was so very sorry for her past actions, but her doubts were overcoming her desires. The more scenarios she thought of, the more she found herself thinking this was a bad idea; however, there was something pushing and prodding her to go.

Her cab pulled up outside her residence. The driver beeped his horn several times, and she went to the door, waving as if to say, 'I'm ready. Just a moment!' She checked the house once more to be sure every light was off and she hadn't forgotten anything she needed. Satisfied all was right, she put on the alarm, opened the door, wheeled her luggage out, and shut the door. She looked at the cabbie, hoping he would come up the walkway and carry some of her things. He didn't, so she trudged back to pick up her flowered valise after leaving the rest of the luggage by the trunk for the cab driver to stow. The man's actions did not please her, and she decided, right there and then, not to tip him.

The hell with that boob! He deserves a bad day.

Comfortably seated in the back of the car, she checked her watch to be sure she had enough time. She knew she did, but it was just a habit of hers. The driver never talked to her after acknowledging she wanted to go to the airport and the Air USA terminal. This was all right with her. Conversations with cab drivers always seemed so forced, and she often flat ran out of things to say and was embarrassed. Small talk was not her forte, but in her business, she had developed the ability to do so; however, she always felt it was strained. Her customers didn't think so, and that was okay with her.

Once at the terminal, the miserable attempt to get everything together began, and she marched the long distance to the check-in area for Air USA Flight 2222. As usual, there were thousands of people moving in all directions, each one cloaked in their own world. Once at the ticketing area, she had to accept and navigate all the hoops that had been laid out for her to jump through just to get a boarding pass, other passenger's complaining under their breath, and the long distances to trudge while carrying her over-zealously packed carry-on. Finally, having endured the long TSA line, she was singled out for the pat down.

How downright embarrassing is this?

Finally, she reached Gate 47, dropped her carry-on as if it were a sack of potatoes and flopped into a seat to wait.

~~ ~~ ~~

After a while, it was announced that Air USA Flight 2222 from Miami to Buenos Aires was delayed one hour, much to the anger of many of the passengers but comfort for Frank who was anxiously fumbling through his briefcase for his ticket. He had already searched his carry-on and was, once again, probably showing a panicked expression. Much to his relief, as he slid his hand down one of the slots between the separators in his case, he touched the familiar airline envelope containing his ticket and boarding passes.

Can't I ever keep the damn tickets in one place so I can always know where they are? Am I some kind of stupid?

He cringed knowing Kate would have given him her usual smirk when he lost something only to find it just where he had put it. He took a deep breath and placed the tickets in his shirt pocket so he would not lose them again. He grinned as the tickets rubbed against his square chin.

Can't lose them now.

Memories of lost tickets flooded his brain, reminding him of the time his boarding pass fell out of his coat in the x-ray machine. He'd reached the gate and had no ticket. He knew it must have happened in the machine, but the attendant said there was nothing in the shute. He'd had to exit the TSA area and go to the ticketing booths again, where he was told the TSA people had found it in the x-ray machine. That necessitated going through the TSA line again. The height of his anxiety had mounted with each slow movement of the line and some confused passengers making it worse. He'd just made the flight boarding. Then he recalled another memory of the time he'd gone to the bathroom with his ticket and when he'd returned to his waiting area seat, the ticket was gone. He'd searched the bathroom without finding the ticket and had to buy a new one. Unfortunately, he couldn't remember the original seat number so he couldn't see who'd picked up his ticket for that flight. He'd cursed himself and whomever had stolen his boarding pass.

~~ ~~ ~~

Helen, seated across from a rather harried-looking man, looked up from the novel she was attempting to read and watched his antics with amusement. As he raised his head, she chuckled, and their eyes met. For a moment, Helen's inner struggle had been interrupted by the man's actions. She sat up and tried to casually straighten her dress so that her pudginess wouldn't show. The man smiled and shrugged, signaling he had everything under control. She lowered her head a bit, raised her eyebrows, and nodded toward his feet where a small purple bag lay to the right of his shoe. He again smiled and nodded, leaned over, and picked up the little bag and put it back into his pocket, pulled out a newspaper he had been sitting

on, and began to read. He appeared embarrassed by this small incident, which had given the impression of him being a klutz.

Helen pretended to return to her book but kept taking peeks at him out of the corner of her eye. He was amusing yet interesting, but the ring on his finger was a prominent feature she couldn't miss.

The announcement for boarding their flight seemed shrill to both of them as they suddenly jerked their heads up simultaneously. Again, smiles came across their faces as they realized their reactions to the common words beginning to emanate from the loud speaker above them. The usual boarding information was announced with those with disabilities or children being allowed to board first, then the airline's members, the first-class passengers, and the group numbers of economy customers.

They began to gather their things, Helen sitting on the edge of her seat and the man leaning back with his carry-on on his lap. He glanced down, maybe to be sure the tickets were still in his shirt pocket, and reflexively touched the envelope. As he looked up, Helen gave him the okay sign with her thumb and forefinger, creating a 'O'. He chuckled, she grinned, and the two stood up at the sound of their group number being called.

Chapter Two

Captain Billy Swanson and Joseph Crenshaw were in the briefing room catching up on the flight plan for Flight 2222 to Argentina. They had known each other from previous flights for quite a while now. Billy was older, but he had always been impressed with Joe's ability and was glad to see him as his first officer. The readouts had been printed out and showed nothing irregular, and the weather over Miami was terrific with minimal winds and no difficult conditions identified. The long-term weather report over South America was to be stormy but nothing they hadn't encountered in their combined thirty-six years of flying. The delay was a simple precaution because one of the baggage ULD's (Unit Load Devices) in the rear bay was not sliding properly, and regulations dictated a specific delay after the problem had been corrected. If the issue was worked out in the right way, the passengers would be boarded. All of this was routine.

While waiting, both of the pilots made their customary inspection of the exterior of their Airbus 330. After each had walked his designated route, they conferred and agreed all was well. They returned to the briefing room, had coffee, and sat in lounge chairs to await their pre-boarding checklist inspection.

The relief pilot, Jane Hodges, appeared in the doorway. "Hey, we gotta problem?"

"ULD's acting up. Be fixed in a jiffy, you know," Billy replied.

Jane walked to the printed flight plans and reviewed them studiously. She then checked and rechecked on the weather, as did her companions just fifteen minutes before.

"Weather's okay until we hit the equator, eh?" Jane asked.

"Yeah, but it might well change a whole lot before we get there. Could be the usual lightning and whatnot," Billy said.

"You gentlemen already done checking the outside?" Jane asked, taking another look at the weather documents.

"Yep, you gonna do the same?"

"Oh yeah. Don't trust you oafs," Jane said, smiling with a twinkle in her eye.

~~ ~~ ~~

Jane exited the room to descend the stairs to the tarmac where she, too, would check every last detail of the exterior of the 330. She stopped to talk to one of the three mechanics working in the rear bay. She showed no undue reaction to what they told her. She continued her walk around the aircraft, waving back at the men as they watched the baggage slowly and smoothly enter the hull.

Jane returned to the briefing room. All six flight attendants for Flight 2222 had arrived, had gone through their pre-flight routines, and were getting ready to enter the plane to prepare the inside for the passengers. Polite pleasantries were exchanged, and everyone went on their way when given the okay that the ULD was now fully functional. The pilots were the last to leave the room, both grabbing another cup of coffee to take with them.

With nine Air USA employees on board as well

as the caterer's team, a few mechanics checking the emergency lighting system, and two passenger liaisons performing their appointed duties, there was no time for foolishness. All were professionals, and nothing was left to chance. This had been drummed into their heads ever since entering this line of work.

One mistake or one thing overlooked could make the difference in any flight whether you were a novice mechanic or a seasoned pilot. They all relied on each other and double, even triple-checking, didn't hurt.

Billy said he was satisfied with everything he had seen, signed the flight release, and got the passenger count and the pre-departure clearance form. They were ready for pushback anytime now.

~~ ~~ ~~

"Good evening. Boarding for Flight 2222 to Buenos Aires will begin shortly. Please have your boarding passes and tickets readily available as you enter the walkway. We will start boarding first-class passengers, those with small children, and those with disabilities, and those of you who need more time than usual to get seated. After that, we will start at the rear of the plane calling out groups of seat numbers. Please check the boarding passes for your seat number and group number so we may board everyone comfortably. Should you need assistance, please let us know here at the desk."

Frank smiled when the announcement referred to filling the plane from the back. Most airlines filled from the front, making it more difficult for people to board, especially those who took their time to stow their gear. He always hated those people who brought on a carry-on that would obviously never fit in the overhead bins but would stand there for eternity shoving and pushing their monstrosity while people piled up behind them. Boarding from the back seemed logical, but Frank knew there were always people who would try to beat the system by placing their carry-ons up front to get them more easily as they left the plane.

If only they would all just adhere to the conventional 'carry-on near one's seat' policy, things would go so much smoother.

Frank, the woman he'd seen reading her book, and the rest of the passengers began checking their passes, gathering their carry-ons and briefcases in anticipation of boarding without any hassle. There seemed to be an underlying exhilaration in everyone, each passenger having a different reason for their excitement.

Chapter Three

Frank watched as the attendants welcomed every passenger with "Good evening", "Hello", or "Welcome Aboard", checked the boarding passes, and pointed in the direction of their seats. The Airbus 330 had four seats in the middle with an aisle on each side separating them from two seats to the far left and right, one window and one aisle. Each seat had a monitor above the tray table for videos, movies, and the usual government-mandated flight instructions. In the pocket below the tray table were the monthly magazine of the airline and an in-flight catalogue with inflated prices. Accompanying them were the ever-present white bag for flight sickness and notices espousing the great advantages with the airline's credit card and how to use their hot spot Wi-Fi.

As usual, some passengers got on at the wrong time; some were in the incorrect aisle for their lettered seats, some hurrying to stow their items so as not to interfere with the others, and some not bothering or just ignoring the passengers trying to get to their seats. Lines built up on each side of the aisles, and it became incumbent upon the attendants to help straighten out the bottlenecks.

And I thought boarding from the back was a great idea.

One such oblivious traveler was a lanky, twenty-or-so-year-old kid with pierced ears and a scraggly goatee. Every bit of his face seemed to have sharp edges—his brow, his nose, his cheekbones, and chin. He was wearing a dyed T-shirt that he'd probably made in his bathroom, stained blue jeans, and green sneakers. His arms were tattooed from the back of his hands to under the short sleeves of his shirt. A prominent red tattoo of what appeared to be a dragon's head on the back of his neck seemed to be peeking over the shirt's thin collar. He stood in the aisle trying his best to shove a large bulging duffle bag into the overhead bin. Anyone with an elementary school education would know from the size of the bag compared to the bin, there was no way it would fit, but not this guy. Frustrations rose geometrically as he continued to push and shove.

"Hey, mon. It ain't gonna fit," a dark-skinned man, holding his three-year-old daughter's hand, said in a Haitian accent.

It made no difference to the hippy creature now obsessed with his bag. It was as if he were deaf. Finally, an attendant appeared, gently explaining that he needed to check his oversized bag and make room for the other people. He argued awhile, but, finally seeing the rest of the passengers becoming increasingly upset with him, concurred with a huffy attitude and moved a few rows to the back of the plane where his seat was. He sat while the attendant retrieved his sack protruding from the overhead bin and started dragging it forward past the other passengers as they slid to the side of the aisle to let her by. She later returned and handed him his baggage check that he quickly and annoyingly grabbed and stuffed into his shirt pocket. Scenes such as this occurred in other areas, but this one was the most egregious without a doubt.

Frank was three people behind the guy. If the man hadn't spoken up, Frank was about to do so. "Idiot," he mumbled. He imagined his facial expression was one of anger, and he purposely eyed the seated dolt. He was not the only one who looked disdainfully at the man, but unfortunately, this person remained totally unaware of the irritated group of people near him.

Great way to start this long trek, Vomit Green Sneaker Man! At the least, you should have put

your damn bag near your seat, a-hole hippy!

Being a seasoned traveler, Frank found his seat, stowed his luggage, and slipped his briefcase under the seat then sat in one fluid motion. His movements were quick and deliberate, but no one seemed to notice. Frank glanced back at the hippy, trying to corral his instinct to give the guy a piece of his mind, but experience had taught him not to do so.

Early in his career, Frank had once been in a similar situation when some dope stood in the aisle fiddling with his luggage for the longest time, totally unaware that a woman with her child in tow stood waiting for him to move aside. He'd continued playing with his luggage in the overhead bin as if taunting the woman. He was a dark-skinned, foreign-looking man wearing sunglasses, standing about six foot and taking up the entire aisle. The woman had been polite and waited even though the child was getting a bit fidgety. Finally, Frank had spoken up from his seat behind the man and told him to let the lady by, and he was met with a torrent of loud vulgarity that instinctively made Frank rise up out of his seat. The man shoved him backward as he'd continued his verbal onslaught. Frank had caught his balance, grabbed his coat, and punched him in his gut. The man had doubled over, coughing. Soon, passengers from the surrounding seats were up and holding both of them from continuing their battle. The attendants called the airport police, and they were soon taking both of them off the plane and interrogating them. Frank had missed that flight and learned a lesson never to interfere unless absolutely necessary.

~~ ~~ ~~

Helen was pulling her poorly weighted carry-on, fighting its determination to flip against the sides of the aisle seats. She had to lift it upright multiple times to continue at a reasonable pace down the narrow aisle not far from where the man she'd seen earlier sat. Her luggage bumped into some hippy's elbow, and he reacted as a child would and flipped it back, almost bouncing it off the passenger across from him. Several other passengers helped set the bag upright, and she was grateful to them for their assistance. She finally arrived at her appointed destination, 24B, next to 24A, the seat belonging to the harried man she'd encountered before.

She watched with a thankful sigh while he rose quickly and lifted her bag up into the bin without asking and made a motion inviting her to take the window seat if she desired. She declined, and he slid back into his seat.

Helen sat, placed her purse under the seat, glanced at the man, and said, "Thank you. It's been quite a trip already."

"Yes, it has, hasn't it. Hopefully more serene after take-off, eh?" he remarked, straightening his tie and pulling down on his sleeve.

"Yeah, sure, more serene. That would be welcomed, for sure," Helen said.

~~ ~~ ~~

Several minutes passed. Frank sensed a fearful attitude in the woman with whom he would have the pleasure or displeasure of being paired for the duration of the overnight flight. She probably hadn't been on an airplane much in her life. He would strike up a conversation with her later. Right now, it was best to let her relax and get her bearings. It wasn't the first time he'd had a 'white knuckler' next to him. He understood their fears, but if the truth be told, they had very little to worry about. Horror stories always have a way of becoming the norm, but statistics proved the opposite.

When the final trickling of the late passengers ended, the entry doors closed. Some people were still moving about collecting their items from their carry-ons and closing the bins. An announcement over the intercom system told everyone to be seated, fasten their seat belts, stow their seat tables in an upright and locked position, and watch the brief video regarding the safety elements of the Airbus 330.

The audio droned on past Frank's ears but was the center of intense attention for the woman beside him. She watched the video intently, almost absorbing every word as her eyes darted back and forth scrutinizing the motions of the actors, especially when the seat belt and water emergency instructions were presented. What was amusing to Frank was the seats in which the actors were seated. They were nothing like the ones they had been assigned to. The video showed spacious distances between the 'passengers' yet, in reality, that was certainly not the case. Economy seating was not roomy, for sure.

A shoehorn should be in the pocket along with the white vomit bag.

The video monitors then returned to their nooks in the ceiling. Frank tried relaxing in the upright position, but he saw his female companion was still on the edge of her seat, fumbling with her seat belt. He calmly reached over and found the longer of the two straps and unraveled it so she could then click it into the buckle in her right hand. She pulled gently on the belt, wiggled a bit to be sure she could breathe, and then appeared to try to seem relaxed, but she really wasn't at all. She nodded to Frank in thanks, not saying a word.

Another broadcast from the senior flight attendant was heard, outlining the food and beverage deliveries throughout the flight. The movie was announced. Frank had already seen it twice on other international flights, but the woman became alive, reaching for her purse to find some dollars for the headset. It was way too early for the payment, but Frank didn't mention it as the attendants came by one last time, checking the seats and making sure all passengers had their belts fastened.

"Attendants, please prepare for take-off."

Frank felt the woman stiffen a bit in her seat. Again, he said or did nothing to console his neighbor.

The usual silence in the cabin occurred with this statement.

~~ ~~ ~~

The 330 taxied onto the runway and made its way behind a jumbo 747. It was seventh in line to take off. Inside the cockpit, Captains Swanson, first officer Crenshaw, and second officer Hodges were performing their final check and recheck of all systems. Everything was right for take-off. The giant engines then raised their decibel levels to a high roaring pitch as the 330 increased speed down the runway to enter the evening sky. The last irregular clatter of the plane against the tarmac disappeared, the whirring of the landing gears entering their compartments with a clunk was heard, and a residual thrumming underneath finally stopped, allowing no more evidence of take-off but a calming hum, the only sound remaining in the cabin.

~~ ~~ ~~

Frank glanced over at the woman without moving his head. Her eyes were wide open during take-off but became normal as the steady sound of flight began. It was obvious to him that she would react to every out-of-the-ordinary noise while the aircraft rose into the sky and gradually leveled off. Frank watched the lights of the city become smaller and disappear into darkness. He had seen this phenomenon many times, but it always mesmerized him to the point that he never missed it on any flight at night. He tilted his head back and closed his eyes. An image of Kate turning to her left and wiggling her butt on their porch appeared in his mind. Her forced smile when he left always had him feeling guilty, but he reminded himself of his position and what he had to do for the firm. If it were his choice, he would send someone else, but he could only wait until the day when he could choose a person such as himself.

He then turned and looked intently at his surroundings. It was a routine game of his, picking certain passengers and trying to guess who they were. Were they listening to the instructions? Did they really know where the oxygen mask was? How old were they? What did they do for a living? Did they have family? What were their likes and dislikes? He never found out the real answers, but selecting a number of people and going through the machinations of figuring out all he could think of passed the time until he could fall asleep, a task he always found daunting. One of them was that inconsiderate hippy dude. Frank knew he was a loner and trouble in someone's life. He was glad not to have to deal with that moron.

Chapter Four

"Good evening, ladies and gentlemen. We have now leveled off at thirty-seven thousand feet. Our flight time to Buenos Aires will be ten hours and thirty-six minutes. The weather seems to be very nice for the first part of the trip, but after passing the equator, we may have some turbulence. This is not unusual on this run. We will keep you informed of our progress as we get nearer to our destination. Now, please sit back and enjoy your meals and entertainment. Thank you for flying Air USA."

The woman beside Frank hung on every word. He noted her reaction and smiled at her.

"A heck of a mouthful, eh?" Frank said.

"Yeah, it's hard to believe we are five miles above the earth," she said and leaned over to look out the window. "It's almost dark. Those clouds over the water are beautiful."

Actually, six-point-nine miles. And we are still breathing," Frank jested.

"Whatever. We're really way up here, aren't

we?"

"Yes. You know there is a group of people who believe that planes are not able to fly whatsoever?"

"Really? How's that?"

"Well, they think there's a movie being shown on a screen outside each window, giving the impression that one is flying, and somehow the plane is being juggled around and noises made to convince the passengers they are flying," Frank replied.

"You're kidding me, right? What do they think when they are in another city when they land?"

"I guess they haven't figured that out yet." He laughed.

She let out a laugh, too, and seemed to be more relaxed in her seat. Frank ended the conversation and pulled out his newspaper. To be sure she was okay, he glanced over at her as she turned toward him.

"Thanks," she said.

He nodded and returned to his paper.

The attendants started the beverage run. The soft sound of passengers talking among themselves was comforting and soothing as the woman ordered a ginger ale. Frank ordered a Diet Coke without ice. No sooner did they get the cups to their lips did a commotion begin with the hippy guy a few rows up, complaining about his mixed drink being watered down. Several attendants were necessary to quiet him. Everyone around this section shook their head in disgust. To shut him up, he was given an extra miniature bottle of vodka.

"There are so many of these idiots around," Frank said.

"Well, he probably has had a miserable life," the woman replied.

"No reason for him to make everyone else miserable, you know."

"He doesn't even know he is." She sighed.

The wisdom and ease with which she'd said that struck Frank as strange. He suddenly wanted to know more about her. She obviously wasn't a time-tested passenger.

"So, what brings you to Argentina?" he asked.

"A family matter."

"Yeah, you got family there?"

"So to speak. A death in the family," she said.

"Sorry to hear that. I'm Frank. You?"

"Oh, Helen. Helen Hampton," she said, turning toward him.

"Hampton doesn't sound Argentinian."

Helen obviously waited for him to continue on. Frank was speechless for a second or two, expecting her to speak.

"Uh, Mason, Frank Mason," he said, somewhat embarrassed that he didn't tell her his last name right away.

"Doesn't sound Spanish, either." Helen giggled.

They both laughed, and each took a sip from their cups.

"Excuse my prying, but I can see you are a bit nervous on a plane," Frank said.

"That would be an understatement. I haven't flown a lot, but I have flown, and it's always tough for me," she answered.

"Well, let me give you a few facts to allay your fears. First, flying is actually the safest mode of transportation. In fact, the odds of a plane crash are one for every one-point-two million flights, with odds of dying one in eleven million. Your chances of dying in a car or traffic accident are one in five thousand. Did you know a plane is safer than a train?"

"My, my, you do know something about planes."

"Well, then, you may want to know some other trivia. Some people think all the passengers are sucked out of an airplane by a through-and-through hole occurring, like a gunshot or something. They think the hole gets larger and larger, but that's not so. A small hole doesn't become larger. A big hole doesn't get bigger, either. If the hole was big enough, only the people right next to the hole would be sucked out if they weren't wearing seat belts or decided to look out to see what was going on," Frank said with a laugh.

Helen giggled, too, and said, "Wow, I didn't know that."

"Here's another. Did you know that the pilot and copilot have at least one hundred checks to go through before getting it off the ground?"

"I guess that's why they get the big bucks." Helen rubbed her thumb over her fingers.

"You've seen the movies when the cockpit goes bonkers when all sorts of buzzers and alarms go off and there's chaos? Not true. Just a light and a mechanical voice occurs on most aircraft to let the pilots know to be alert. There's no buzzer or light that screams 'Mountain!'"

"Not a button for an alarm for 'Goose' either, I guess."

"Yep, no honk, honk 'Goose' alarms, either."

"Darn," she said.

"Movies create impossible crashes just to scare people, and now people think they occur all the time. Truthfully, most accidents occur at take-off or landing, and they aren't that exciting when visualized. Now, I'm sure the people inside have visions of some movie they saw, but that's not usually the case."

"Hum, informative, aren't we?" Helen said.

"Did you know some people think the oxygen in the masks makes you euphoric so you don't care what's going on? Stupid people only, that is. And some think the crash position is only a conspiracy to keep your teeth from injury so they can identify you later."

"Okay, now you're getting ridiculous." Helen sat up and stared at him with a smile.

"But you are more relaxed now, aren't you. All of this nonsense has taken your mind off the plane ride."

"You are one sneaky passenger. Have you done this before?" Helen asked.

"Not often, only to help people out of their fears, I guess."

"Well, you done did a good job. Thanks."

"On another subject, I have a game I play on these long trips. It helps spend the time and challenge your thinking powers. Want to play along?"

"Another bunch of plane trivia?

"Nope."

"What's that, then?" she asked.

"I pick out seven people and try to figure how old they are, what nationality they are, what kind of job they have, what their names are and whether they are married or not, kids, personality traits, and anything else I can think of."

"Why seven?" Helen asked.

"Gosh, I have no idea. It has always been seven, I guess. No reason really."

"Okay, begin with jerko over there." She laughed, pointing at the scraggly hippy.

"Well, he is definitely single," Frank blurted, almost spitting out his drink.

Helen leaned forward in convulsive laughter, spilling her drink on her dress. Still chuckling, she wiped her skirt with her napkin. "Duh!" she finally whispered. "Don't do that again. That was really funny."

"Hey, it's got to be true, right?"

"Yup. What else?" she asked, becoming more excited about the game. "Of course, there could have been another flower child who was stupid enough to marry this whacko, and it probably lasted two or three weeks."

"Now you're getting into the game. He's probably part Greek and part Irish. He has to be a busboy somewhere. He can't have the smarts to be anything but." After placing his thumb and index finger on his chin, Frank said, "Ah, let's see. His name is...Homer."

"No way! He's a Herbert. That's why he is so angry. He's had that hanging over him all his life. So, he's miserable. I think he's a student. Probably got all C's in his junior year. Community college, though, works part time as a computer programmer. The other part is spent teeing people off," she said.

"Really? He has a brain? Come on! Let's get real. Oh, we're really close on this one." Frank raised his eyebrows. "This idiot has to be doing some cubicle job where he relates to no one but himself. He probably never communicates with real people in his job. His inner self is the center of his world. A hamburger flipper named Homer, not Herbert."

"Well, I have to agree with you there. I'd like to smack him upside the head and straighten him out. Who's next?" Helen asked, sitting up higher to choose someone.

Her remark was somewhat surprising to Frank. He didn't think she was so adamant about this jerk's actions, but it was obvious she was much more turned off by them than he was, and he was really disgusted by him.

I sense a bit of anger, possibly vindictiveness here, little lady.

"How about that gentleman with the coat and tie on, handkerchief in his coat pocket?" Frank suggested.

"Oh, that's too easy," she said confidently.

"Excuse me, what would you like for dinner? We are serving beef or chicken," an attendant interrupted. She was a redhead with a short haircut, slender to the point of being skinny, but with a pleasant smile and manner about her. Her uniform outlined her shapely body nicely.

Frank noticed the name, Kimberly, on her brass tag pinned to her blue and white Air USA blouse.

"Helen?" Frank offered her the first response.

"Chicken, please."

"I'll have the beef. Thanks, Kimberly."

The attendant raised her eyes to meet his and smiled, wrote the order down, repeating, "24A, beef, and 24B, chicken," and moved on.

They couldn't agree what their new target's

background was. Helen guessed the man was a CEO of a large corporation, probably steel or oil. He was definitely Jewish, not married, possibly a widower, no children, and somewhere between fifty and fifty-five in age. Frank offered Mosha as his name. Helen vehemently disagreed, naming him Irving.

"Ugh! How bad can you be? Irving? Why not Julius or Shalom?"

"So what's his real background, smarty?" Helen jokingly asked.

"Okay, he was, uh, let's see, uh, one of those Special Forces guys when younger. You know, in the Israeli army. Tough as nails. Not sure he has a family. There, that good enough?"

"Oh my God, you really are into this silly game of yours." Helen giggled and smirked at Frank. "No way, Frank. Special Forces? Where did you pull that one from? He's too skinny and frail to have been in such an elite outfit, but he looks wiry enough to have been one a while back, I guess."

Once again, Helen impressed Frank with her intuition.

Chapter Five

Dinner was served without fanfare. The movie was playing, and Helen had donned her headset. She was chewing on her chicken a bit longer than one should, giving Frank a feeling of satisfaction with his choice. His beef was tender, but there was not much of it. The cursory cookie and cake for dessert was minimally tasteful but easily consumed. As he glanced toward his companion, a polite smile creased her face. Half of the cake remained on her plate. The cookie had not been touched. Frank reached for the call button, pushed it, and waited.

"You rang?" another attendant asked. She was older and more seasoned than Kimberly. Her demeanor was all professional. No smile, no specific eye contact.

"Please, two Kaluha and milks on the rocks, here."

"Sure, that will be twelve dollars. And I'll be back in a minute with the drinks."

Frank inched forward in his seat, removed his

seat belt, reached into his pocket to retrieve his billfold, and produced the exact change. The woman thanked him and left. Kimberly eventually returned with the drinks, a sight welcomed by Frank.

She set one in front of Helen, who was surprised. She removed her ear pieces just in time to hear the attendant ask," Anything else for you two?"

"No, thank you," Helen answered before Frank had a chance to say a word. "Thank you for the after-dinner drink, or should I say after-whatever-that-meat-was drink," she said.

"No problem. My pleasure." Frank chuckled. "So, not a tender massaged and coddled Perdue chicken, eh?"

"You could say that chicken had been in some kind of rough boot camp too long."

They sipped their drinks in silence, both of them checking out who they would choose next as their choice in Frank's game. He continued to suck on the ice at the bottom of his plastic container, trying to get every bit out of his six dollars as he watched the movie progress without sound. This was another activity he used to pass the time on long flights, guessing what was being said by reading the character's lips. He had no experience in reading lips, but it was a challenge to try. He thought he was getting pretty good at it, but there were times when he had no inkling what they were saying.

He turned and raised his head to scan the nearby passengers to begin the guessing game again but found Helen fast asleep, the headset cockeyed across her forehead. He removed it gently. A soft glow from the cabin lights illuminated her face. She was not especially pretty—plump cheeks, non-conforming lips, and eyes that were slightly uneven—but there was something about her that interested Frank. It wasn't sexual at all. She seemed to be alluring in another, more intellectual way.

Sleep tight, little lady. Wish I could sleep on a flight.

He had spent many an hour on an airplane, big ones, little ones, and puddle jumpers. He had tried multiple ways to get some shut-eye, but everything he did was a failure. It seemed as if these methods got the opposite effect: alcohol, sleeping pills, non-narcotic sleeping aids, and even counting sheep. None of these worked. He had tried some of the sleeping aids he'd seen in the ever-present catalog in the pocket in front of him and those in the airport shops: neck pillows, sleep blinders, multiple-shaped pillows for window seats, but they turned out to be a waste of money. With his head tilted against the soft small airline's pillow, he stared out into the night, counting the red blinking light at the end of the wing.

Red sheep! Damn, one o'clock, and I don't feel a bit sleepy. Oh, well, might as well hit the head.

Seat belt unhooked, he climbed in slow motion over Helen's outstretched legs until he was firmly in the aisle. To his left sat an elderly woman still adorned with a hat that could have been worn by a movie star in the 1930s. She didn't seem to be that ancient, but the long dress, thick hose, and broad-based heels certainly added up. Yep, she had to be at least in her eighties, retired piano teacher, born in the good old USA, probably of British descent. Her name would be Maxine. She looked like a Maxine, and with her supposed British background, Frank thought this name would definitely be appropriate.

Let's see what Helen comes up with.

Dodging legs and feet in the aisle, he made his way to the rear of the plane. Kimberly was there going over paperwork when Frank arrived. Because of his many sleepless nights on aircrafts, he had a great familiarity with this section of the airplane.

"Anything I can do for you?" she whispered.

"Water would be fine. Nothing else will help me sleep, right?" He was hoping this question would create a magic answer from her or, at least, an opening for a conversation to pass the time.

"Sure." She filled a coffee cup with bottled water and handed it to him then returned to her paper chores.

Frank dallied in the rear for another three to four minutes, drinking slowly. He then waited for one of the bathroom doors to open and entered into the cramped cubicle. *Ah, Homer would love to be in here, wouldn't he? Just the right size for a Mr. Narcissist to live.* After relieving himself and using the mirror to loosen his shirt and tie, he returned to his seat. Helen was awake and moved her legs gently aside to let him in.

"So, can't sleep, eh? Want to continue the game?" she inquired.

He was never so happy to hear those words. "Sure, I can't sleep anyway. You begin."

"Okay. How about that guy?"

She pointed to a rather heavy-set, round-faced bearded man slouched in his seat. His tie was loosely fitted around his enormous bulging neck, sporting a thick, ballooning double chin. His hair rested irregularly on his head, highly suggesting a toupee gone awry. His arms extended well over the armrest, and he looked as if someone had tried to shove a round object into a square hole and succeeded in doing so. He was snoring with abrupt deep breaths followed by times of silence and then followed by a coughing episode. His neighbors were visibly annoyed.

"Um, let's see," Frank said. "Fifty-two and married. Three kids. Salesman, named Ernie. Irish, Scottish descent. Alcoholic, maybe. Definitely sleep apnea."

"Nope. I agree with the age, but I think he owns a bar, maybe a few of them, divorced. Okay on the three kids, I guess. His name has to be Otto. Definitely of German descent. Too much spaetzle and potato pancakes in his diet," Helen said.

"Spaetzle? You mean those little German dumplings or noodles? Hmmm, could be, but I think you're wrong. You could be so far off here. I'm going to win going away, Helen."

"How do you know you win? Do you interview these people after the flight?" she queried.

"No. Never see them again. Just a game to pass the time away."

"Then don't tell me you win," she said without taking her eyes off him.

"Damn, you are serious about this," he said, raising his eyebrows and pointing his finger at her.

"You know I'm going to win," she said, laughing at his intent look.

"All right then. The game is on, girl!" Frank said. "Who's next?"

"That couple there. Honeymooners, no doubt. Twenty-five for the woman and twenty-nine for the man. She's a secretary, and he is in graduate school. His or her parents are paying for the trip. Nationality is an easy one. He's Japanese and she Asian. Her name is...let's say Soo Mi. I had a Korean at work by that name," Helen rattled off.

"Well, I can agree with most of what you said. Her facial contour definitely is Asian. He could be Korean, but I'm voting for Japanese, definitely a Yuto for the guy's name. One more," Frank said, smiling.

"Really? Yuto? So lame! Where did you get that name?"

"Well, it is one of the most popular Japanese names. Y-U-T-O."

"My, my, you sure know a lot. I would have never come up with a real name for him."

"So, we have one more?"

"Let's see. Jerko, the Jewish man, the heavy guy...the honeymooners, that's only five. Wow, there's two more," Helen said, counting on her fingers.

Realizing he had picked one already, Frank remarked, "Well, I did get one while you were

Thomas Neviaser

asleep."

"Who?" Helen asked, looking around the side of her seat.

"That elderly lady across the aisle, down about four rows."

Helen turned her head to look into the aisle, glanced down and spied the woman. "So?"

"Eighties, retired piano teacher, British, Maxine," Frank quickly said.

"No way, Jose. Late seventies, retired but a private secretary for a corporate executive, and she is not a Brit. Italian, for sure, and her name would be...uh... Sofia. On second thought, maybe you have the upper hand here. Now that I see her profile better, definitely English. Piano teacher, maybe, who knows. Love the name Maxine. Gotta go with that."

"That's only six people. Jerko, Israeli man, Maxine, the heavy guy, and the married couple. We need one more to complete the game," he said, somewhat amazed that Helen had been taken so much by the game. "Okay. Kimberly, attendant, thirties. From Chicago. Danish. There, we're done."

"No, French heritage. Way back, you know," Helen said, yawning and rubbing her eyes. "I guess you're right. Well, at least we do know what her real name is, don't we?" Helen continued to yawn. "I'm really getting heavy eyes, and there isn't anything interesting written on the back of my eyelids to keep me up. Here I go."

"Well, I guess that's it. It has been a pleasure playing with you. I'm going to try to get some shut-eye, but it's going to be tough. Don't let the bedbugs bite," Frank mused.

"Goodnight, Mr. Mason."

"Frank! Goodnight, Ms. Hampton."

Frank glanced over to see her moving her head toward the aisle. She was asleep faster than anyone he had ever seen before. He was so jealous of this ability. He turned to the window, folded the pillow on itself, and pushed his head into it firmly. No sooner had he closed his eyes, he opened them to realign the pillow and shift his body in the seat. This scenario continued off and on for the next twenty minutes, much to his angst. It was as if he had 'restless body syndrome', somewhat akin to the 'restless leg' one. He would wiggle his ankle as fast as he could as if exercising would make him tired. This never helped, but he always tried it. There was not much room on these economy seats to do anything else. Then he tried pumping his knee up and down followed by the other, and then folded his arms across his chest.

Crap! Nothing's happening!

Geez, I hate this.

He thought of Kate again. How was she doing? She should be asleep now. Oh, how he wished he could be by her side. He loved her warm body next to him, and the smell of her hair always captivated him. The warmth of their comforter added to their snuggling, altogether a feeling of safety and love nurturing them until morning. Nothing could make him fall asleep better than his wife by his side and in his own home. With this image in his head, he was actually finally able to fall asleep on a plane for once.

Chapter Six

Captain Swanson and Crenshaw were comfortably seated while Jane Hodges was checking her records of the flight. The big Airbus was on autopilot, and it was time for each to take time out of the cockpit for a bathroom break, a drink, and something to munch on. Billy took the first break, and he nodded to Joe and Jane to take over.

"Everything seems great, don't you think, Joe?" Billy remarked as he left.

"Don't see any problems. Just another routine jaunt, I suspect," Joe said.

Jane moved over to Billy's seat and began to check the instruments. She looked out her window into the beautiful night sky. The low level of lighting in the quarters allowed her to see millions of stars. She motioned to Joe and pointed them out. He smiled and watched for a few moments, leaned back, and closed his eyes.

A small vibration jolted Jane from her vision of the stars. It did not last long, but, to be certain, Jane scanned the entire instrument panel looking for any signs of danger. She saw none, remained vigilant for any minor or unusual oscillation, but relaxed after a few minutes. Then, there was another sound similar to the first, lasting a bit longer. This time, she alerted Joe from his slumber. He perked upright and proceeded to search for any signs of trouble. The jerking sensation soon stopped. Joe and Jane looked at each other, both shrugging it off as the sound had disappeared and the plane was running smoothly.

"I'll tell Billy as soon as he comes back. Couldn't have been turbulence since it seemed to only be on your side of the plane," Joe said. "Anything on your wing?"

Jane leaned forward and visually inspected the left wing. "Everything seems okay there."

As she sat back, a low-pitched thump was audible and felt by Jane.

"Damn, what was that?" Jane snapped.

"Haven't heard anything like that before," Joe responded.

Jane checked the wing. "Not a thing there. The

wing isn't vibrating, the engine shows no sign of a wear, and no smoke or fire."

"Could anything like that sound be coming from the belly of this beast?" Joe asked.

"No freaking idea, Joe," Jane replied.

"Well, it sure is running smooth right now," Joe said, still glancing over the panel in front of him.

Billy soon returned to chewing on a sandwich with a cup of juice in his hand. He stood at the door, discarded his cup, and swallowed his last bite. Jane got up and returned to her seat.

As soon as Billy got into position, Joe said, "We've had some weird noises and vibrations since you left. They didn't last long. One tiny vibration, another one, and a thump. All on the left, it seems. The last could have been left belly. Right, Jane?"

"Yeah, weird, for sure. Never heard that thump before," Jane concurred.

"You say everything's on the left?" Billy asked as he scanned the left wing and partially stood up and looked back to see as much of the junction of the wing and the plane as possible. He started eying each specific instrument in front of him and Joe.

"All seems intact."

Over the next fifteen minutes, no other reverberations or unusual sounds were felt or heard. The crew could only speculate as to the origin of them but were relieved that everything was calm. Jane got up and motioned that she was taking her break.

"Just in, there's storm activity being reported now just east of the islands, mostly over Puerto Rico. Evidently, some lightning and heavy winds, but I think we can avoid it by revising the route more east of P.R. and then get back on course once passed it. What do you think?" Billy asked.

"Seems routine to me. I'm looking at that info right now. Seems to me that we may have to go pretty far east to avoid it all, but I don't see any problem with that decision," Joe responded.

The door to the cockpit opened, and Jane returned to her seat. Billy and Joe both went over the rerouting of the flight pattern with her, and once she concurred, the coordinates were programed into the computer to bypass the weather ahead. An ever so slight banking of the Airbus could be felt as it responded to its instructions. Once it leveled off, Billy placed the A330 on autopilot again and relaxed in his seat, awaiting the next few hours for the usual brilliant sunrise in the east.

~~ ~~ ~~

A yellow hue had now appeared on the eastern horizon. Joe yawned, stretched, unbuckled his seatbelt, and started to get up when a huge tremor followed by a large explosion on the left wing broke the silence. The plane lurched to the left, throwing Joe against Jane as she was just getting her gear on. Billy immediately took control of the plane, switching off the autopilot while Joe was trying desperately to get to his co-pilot position. Jane was pushing him up and forward off her lap so she could be free to help out.

"Transmit our position and keep transmitting. I'm losing control of this bird slowly but surely. We're going down, guys. Let's try to do it so some of us have a chance to survive," barked Billy, fighting desperately with the control yoke and the rudder pedals.

The vibrating aircraft was definitely in trouble. Billy leaned forward and looked out at the left wing. The engine was on fire, and the front half appeared to be severely deformed and charred from the raging flames. He could just make out what seemed to be extensive damage to the wing. Parts of the wing were curled up and flapping as the air passed irregularly over the airfoil.

"Damn, I think we had a compressor blade failure. It's destroyed that engine and cut up the wing big time. This is really screwing with any control over the plane for sure. Some of the engine parts must have penetrated the fuselage, and now we have a fire that's getting bigger and bigger," Billy said in a controlled but worried voice.

"The right engine looks good, but that fire is going to take us down. The fire extinguishing bottles didn't do a thing to that engine fire. We're at thirty-four now," Joe replied.

"I can feel the heat. Keep transmitting. Just keep it up. Joe, notify the attendants and the passengers," Billy said.

Billy set the transponder to 7700, and Jane keyed her microphone repeating, "May Day, May Day, May Day, Air USA twenty-two twenty-two. I repeat, May Day, May Day, May Day, Air USA Flight twenty-two twenty-two. Left engine explosion, fire, and losing altitude."

~~ ~~ ~~

"Everyone, fasten all seat belts, we have no left engine, we will need to ditch into the sea. FASTEN SEAT BELTS! ASSUME CRASH POSITIONS!" a voice bellowed over the intercom system.

The attendants were scurrying up and down the aisle, awakening passengers who did not respond to the orders. Other passengers had been aware of the sudden explosive sound and subsequent relentless rattling and awkward tilting of the aircraft. Screams and audible, fearful voices were increasing in intensity as passengers grasped desperately at the seats in front of them, heads darting every which way to see what others were doing.

~~ ~~ ~~

"Wake up, Frank. Be sure your seatbelts are on and tight," Kimberly said. "We are having tremendous problems right now, be alert. Assume your crash positions. An engine's on fire. We're losing altitude, and we're crash-landing into the sea." Kimberly was shaking Helen and prodding Frank and forcefully speaking to them. "Hurry up!"

Frank's sleep fog evaporated immediately, and they followed her instructions. As Frank leaned over, the early brim of the rising sun beamed through Frank's window, illuminating Helen's terrified face screaming without sounds.

"Duck down!" Frank screeched as a backpack flew out of their overhead bin, just missing her face. He flipped out his left hand to direct the pack to the floor. Some idiot had tried to open an overhead bin to retrieve something. "Goddamn asshole!" Frank muttered.

He unbuckled his seat belt and stood, hunched over Helen's left side. "Hold on to my hand no matter what happens. Now! Grab my belt with your other hand and don't let go."

She clasped her right hand into his outstretched

right hand, squeezing it tightly. Her left hand followed, landing on his side and slipping down past his belt. Frank grabbed her hand and brought it up to just above the belt, loosened his own belt buckle a bit so she could get her fingers under it, and tightened it again. He then sat, flipping the armrest between them up, and clicked his seat belt. All of this was performed in a deliberate and smooth Olympic-style motion.

The chaotic commotion, loud voices conversing with others, and screams of terror were muted by the tilting of the cabin and the increasing shuddering of the plane. Some of the overhead bins popped open, and baggage poured out onto the passengers. The entire plane was starting to tilt downward, well past the angle one would expect for a normal landing. It was like being in a roller coaster that was just about to plunge downward but never straightening out. Frank peered over the bottom of the window to see nothing but sky and the early dawn. It seemed an indeterminable amount of time as the airplane rumbled and tossed in its descent. Looking down, he could just make out the water below slowly rushing up at the left side of the aircraft. The passengers' shrieks and screams were the last thing he heard as he desperately held Helen's hand, and then a terrific forward force into the monitor and tray table...

And then a black silence.

Chapter Seven

Helen's gasping for breath was the first sound Frank heard. Drenched from the flow of water entering the economy section, a foggy vision of his fold-up tray appeared. His right hand was clenched in something so tight he could hardly move his fingers. To his left, water seeped through a crack in the double-pane window, and a level of sea water rose slowly up inside the plastic panel. The heavy coughing and breathing continued to his right, but turning his neck to that side was difficult. Helen's tray seat was open and interposed between Helen and him.

Using all his strength, he bent the tray down, revealing the blood-strewn face of his companion, mouth contorted and eyes wide in terror. The water rose toward her face, her right hand still clasping his. Frank reached to find her other hand still gripping his belt. Unfastening his seat belt was easy, but hers was somehow now crushed by her tray. Struggling to stand and jerking his hand free, he released the tray from her belt and unbuckled her as he lifted her to an upright position.

"Helen, any broken bones?"

"I...I...don't think...so."

"Can you move with me? I see some outside light." Looking for any other way out, he could see limp, lifeless bodies, some in their seats and others floating in the aisle. He glanced from side to side. Some beams of sunlight were evident, but there was only one that seemed to have promise. Peripherally, he witnessed some possible motion among a few passengers urging him to yell, "Go to the light. Up there." He repeated it over and over, pointing to a three-to-four-foot opening where an emergency door on the left side of the aircraft had popped open. "Do it now before more water comes in."

Helen's intermittent weakness was increasing as he lifted and pulled her through the aisle. Her reaction to the debris mixed with baggage and some mangled bodies was deafening. She was getting heavier.

"Get a hold of yourself," Frank said. "It's life or death! Now!"

The emergency door moved slowly, and Frank pushed his back and rear end against it to fully open the hatch door. Across the buoyant chute outside, the right wing of the airplane was half submerged, but areas of temporary safety existed. He pushed harder, then he shoved Helen out in front of him.

"Stay here. Hold on to this," he said, placing her hands on a circular clip on the slide.

She hesitated to let go of his belt and hand, but Frank's determined stare into her eyes made her release both hands, and he guided her left hand to the clip. Reaching the door again, he poked his head inside to see if any other passengers were moving toward the opening. The goatee of the hippy jerk appeared, his face covered by a blanket soaked in blood.

"Help me," said the meek and strained voice of a once obnoxious know-it-all.

Frank reached for his arm and slid it over his shoulder, partially dragging the individual, whose feet and legs were rotating as if he were riding a bike. He laid the man next to Helen and returned to the cabin door. No more people came out. He knelt next to the two survivors on the slide. "Get up on the wing. Now! We have to find something that floats and hang on," he said, frantically looking in all directions for anything substantial.

"Don't let go of me," the hippie said.

"Gotta get more people out. Get yourself up farther on the wing—now," Frank said.

"No, you don't understand. I need help."

"There's a lot of others that need help. Now, help yourself for once."

"Anyone in there?" Frank asked as he turned to the exit doorway.

He searched the inside of the cabin. The arrangement of seats that were so orderly on departure were now a scene of twisted metal and seat covers that in no way resembled what they were. Multiple seats had been ripped from their moorings, some with bodies in them and others empty. Frank had no idea where those people or their bodies were. There was no human movement. The only motion throughout the entire cabin and what he could see of the business-class seats was from baggage, tray tables, and cups floating in the rising, bloody water.

Smoke from some of the electric components in contact with the saltwater was now obscuring his vision. He continually tripped over objects under the water, often having to step up and over what he knew were bodies or soft baggage. He couldn't take time to find out which was which. If they were bodies, they were dead. He gathered up all the life vests he could that were floating but didn't bother to try to get others that were still under the seats. He shoved all of these to the exit door and watched them disappear as the others were putting them on themselves.

Someone yelled back to him, "We have more than enough vests."

Suddenly, behind him, a young couple were hunched over, holding a barely moving body. It was that of the elderly woman a few seats down the aisle. The woman said, "She's breathing, but I don't know..."

Frank guided them out to the wing with an outstretched hand and helped boost the old woman's limp body into his arms and sat back on the wing while turning her face up. Her pale face was shriveled, not just from her aging wrinkles. Sea water spurted from her nose and mouth as she wheezed and breathed the smoky air around the airplane. The man and woman helped shove and then pull the old woman up the wing and, once seated next to Helen, she proceeded to prop the woman's head up on her legs and covered her with her body as well as she could. The couple gathered around her and helped comfort the woman.

Her eyes opened and slowly moved from side to side with her trying to get her bearings and an idea of what type of condition she was in. "Is my purse here?" were the first words she said.

A fleeting smile came across Helen's lips, probably because this question was not what one would expect a person rescued from ocean waters to say.

"No," said Helen.

"Oh, God, my pills, they're gone."

"Diabetes pills?" Helen asked.

"No, cancer. They were helping, you know."

~~ ~~ ~~

Helen held the woman's head closer to her chest and tried to pull her clothing up in an attempt to keep her warm. She thought of Maria and how she could have been this kind and understanding to her during her long period of illness. She dipped her head into the woman's gray wet hair and wept.

~~ ~~ ~~

The sun's blazing heat helped comfort the six survivors as Frank and the young man searched for floatation.

"There, there. Raft there," the man said.

No sooner were the words out of his mouth, the man dove into the sea to retrieve a large yellow emergency raft that somehow must have been dislodged by the emergency door and chute. Holding a loose rope-type handle, he swam side-stroke to the wing and edged the raft against it. One by one, each person was helped into the raft by Frank, and finally the young man swung one leg then the other over the side and entered the raft.

"Large enough for all to stretch out," the man

said with a definite Japanese accent.

"We're going to need water," said Frank.

"Then must go back there?" the man asked, pointing back at the plane's exit hatch.

Frank and the man looked at each other quizzically, Frank realizing they would have to be the ones to get the water they so desperately needed. They swiveled to face the emergency door but hesitated, returning to the tomb of so many others, but, realizing they had no choice, they entered the airplane. With a hand signal, Frank went forward, and the younger man toward the rear. Frank was immediately met with floating limbs, clothes, luggage, and debris from all over the plane. He sloshed through hats, coats, books, cell phones, and other items trying desperately to get to the galley. Once there, he reached the two maroon-colored latches that kept the food carts secure, flipped them to the release position, opened them, and allowed the plastic containers to float out. He started to try to guide them to the emergency exit. The bottles and cartons kept bobbing, rolling, disappearing, and popping back up, making it difficult to push them to the exit.

Meanwhile, the young husband was herding a bunch of bottles of water in a plastic carton he had found to the same exit. Seeing the carton he had, Frank turned and searched for some others like it in his galley. He found two of them stuck between another tray holder and the unopened exit door. He quickly filled them with more dinners, put the other items from the water into the large cartons, and pushed them to the exit door where the man was waiting to retrieve them and get them to the raft. The man grabbed the loose dinners and placed them high on the wing for safety until they could fetch them again.

Suddenly, there was a splashing commotion at the exit door. Another passenger, a dapper, well-dressed man tugging on something huge, appeared at the door. The large item behind him was Otto from Frank's game. Flailing and thrashing his right arm, which was visibly bent in the middle of his forearm, he began to shriek in pain from his broken limb. Water spouted from his mouth as he screeched, causing a mixture of howling and gargling. It took everyone's strength to haul him onto the wing. He was huge and not cooperating very much.

"Jesus," screamed Helen, staring into the water.

A uniformed body, kicking slowly in the water, facedown, was slopping partially under the wing of the airplane in front of them. The dapper man from the game reached out, pulled the body out from under the wing, and turned it over as fluid and blood blew from its mouth.

"Kimberly?" Frank bellowed.

"Help me," she blubbered, hardly getting out the words. Blood was oozing from a gash on the right side of her head.

"Hold on." The stylish man slid her limp body onto the base of the wing and propped her head in his arms, wiping her mouth with his sleeve and tugging mucus from her teeth and the back of her mouth to clear her airway. He cupped his mouth over hers and exhaled a large breath into her lungs. A belching cough brought the motionless body to life, followed by a cacophony of burps, coughs, and wheezes. Her eyes opened, and Kimberly wiped the messy slime from her face with her dress so she could see. She lay motionless for a second or two.

"Anyone alive?" Kimberly managed to speak in a rasping whisper.

"Yeah. Nine of us survived so far. I'm not sure there are any others. The cabin is almost full of water. If they aren't out now, they will never be. Can you get into the raft there?"

"It inflated?" Kimberly asked.

Frank did not expect this question from someone who was trained to know all the emergency aspects of the aircraft but didn't ask for an explanation. He motioned to the young man once again, and they tried to retrieve the carton of water bottles, soft drinks, peanuts, pretzels, and the leftover unused dinners that Frank had saved from the galley as they passed by the door. Anything that could be used was salvaged. Soon, others, who were physically fit enough, helped bring supplies after getting the big man and a disoriented Kimberly in the raft. With her head wrapped in a pillow case, the elderly woman tried to organize items to make room for the survivors. The hippie guy sat shivering and glassy-eyed. No arrogance and wise comments now.

The wing slowly started to disappear into the water, essentially leaving the top of the hull as the only sign of the invalid craft. A few minutes later, the nose tilted down, the tail rose, and the plane sank into the sea in slow motion. No one spoke. The morning sun was now beaming brightly. An amazing silence covered the crash site, the only sound being the waves slopping against the raft and the heavy breathing of all nine survivors—Frank, Helen, and their seven game players.

Chapter Eight

The rhythmic rocking of the boat was hypnotizing. With glassy eyes gazing at the bottom of the raft, onto the horizon or up into the sky, the faces of the remaining nine were stamped in absolute disbelief. Heavy sighs, coughs, and painful moans were the order of the moment. Some stared ahead, others tried unsuccessfully to get comfortable in the crowded raft, and others continued to scan the sea for anything that gave them hope.

"Hopefully help should be here soon. When planes fall off the radar, the location is immediately marked and rescue teams alerted. We're all dehydrated, and there are plenty of water bottles here," the dapper man said. "But don't drink too quickly or a lot fast, people. If we flew way off course, they may never know where we are, and it is going to take a long time to find us. I'd advise not drinking everything so fast. Ration it. It could be a long time before we are rescued."

"Oh, my God, they're not coming?" the heavy man screeched.

"I didn't say that. It may take longer than we want, so we need to be prepared."

"Who the hell are you to be telling us all this?" the big man blurted out, holding his right arm close to his side.

"Good question. I'm Irving. Who are you?"

"My name is Otto."

Helen's attention darted from staring at the floor to meet Frank's undoubtedly quizzical facial expression. He never knew what his game people's names really were, yet...

How the hell can they be their real names?

"My God," Helen stated with disbelief. "Irving, Otto. Did you hear that, Frank?"

Frank turned to the others, not saying a word, yet asking their names.

"Maxine," said the old lady.

This was followed by, "Yuto, my wife Soo Mi."

"Kimberly. I was one of the attendants."

All turned to the hippy guy who had not said a word, knees curled up with his arms clutching his legs to his chest. He looked up at the rest staring at him. "What. What do you want?" After a few seconds, it dawned on him the others wanted to know his name. "Homer," he said.

Frank—and clearly Helen—were totally surprised and in a quandary. They were staring at each other expecting each to have an answer, but there was none forthcoming.

"All these people have the same names we gave them in our game," said Helen, leaning closely against Frank. "That can't be. We don't know any of them. How can this be? You think we've met them before? No, that's impossible."

"Yeah, I know," Frank whispered. He faced the others and said, "I'm Frank, and this is Helen."

"How's this possible?" Helen whisper-screamed.

"God, it's so weird. I haven't a clue, but it is what it is," Frank answered. "Well, introductions aside for now, is anyone badly hurt other than Otto?" he asked.

Helen was still staring at the passengers and back to Frank, seeking some semblance of truth to this mystery.

No one raised their hand. It was a great relief to know they did not have a medical emergency on board. Frank could not get over the fact that all the passengers' names in the game had been correctly guessed by Helen or him. *Jesus, how could that be?* Clairvoyance was not a specialty of his. The amazement of this event was soon shrouded by the next question.

"What the hell are we going to do now?" Otto inquired as he winced in pain.

"Remain calm so as not to utilize all of your strength. Breathe slowly. Sip some water but don't gulp it. Each one of us should keep a lookout in different directions on the raft," Irving stated forcibly while searching the pockets and flaps of the raft.

"What are you doing?" Maxine questioned.

"Some of these floatation devices have emergency beacons, flares, emergency kits, and maybe a flashlight."

That said, everyone but Otto started pulling down any flaps near them and looking. Soo Mi found the beacon and handed it to Irving. The homing beep responded when he flipped the switch. Maxine yelped like a little girl, holding a large flashlight, pointing the bright beam at each person.

"Easy, Maxine. Let's not wear out the battery," Frank said.

"Oh, yeah. Sorry." She turned to hunt for more compartments where anything that could be of help could be hidden.

Kimberly had searched deeper into the pocket from which Maxine had pulled the flashlight to undercover six flares. "Flight school training. I just wasn't thinking. I should have told you immediately," she said, holding them above her head.

"Not that you have anything on your mind. Don't worry about it," Frank responded.

A calm finally came over the group with the discovery of the emergency items. All breathed a sigh of obvious relief. Each turned in a different direction as instructed by Irving and scanned the sea and sky. What Frank saw was not the serenity of a calm ocean such as one seen on television in the ads for tropical islands. What he saw was endless water and small waves seemingly multiplying one after the other as if an audience watching the raft. The horizon was flat, dead flat. The only comforting aspect of it was that the sun's rays allowed them some warmth from the cold and damp condition they were in. There were no shadows on the water or in the sky to give them any hope of immediate rescue.

Initially, they all appeared focused, intently watching in a continuous fashion. However, after an hour or so, the enthusiasm waned, and people nodded and stared emptily at the bottom of the raft. As the hours wore on, only a few lifted their heads to study the water. The sound of the water beating against the raft was only outweighed by the homing device.

Beep...beep...beep...

Chapter Nine

The sun was setting, and a cool breeze had begun to blow. Frank awoke to see Yuto and Soo Mi staring at the sea, then splashing their faces with seawater. Helen's head was lying in Frank's lap, the back of her head blood-caked. He soaked a rag with water and attempted to moisten the blood to remove it. She tried to open her eyes, but the seawater mist had evaporated, and a salty crust covered her eyelids. Frank dabbed the rag on her eyes gently.

"Thanks. Any signs of...?" Helen whispered.

"No. They'll be here soon."

"How do you know?" she asked.

"Hey, this is the twenty-first century. Technology and all that stuff. They know we're down. They will search for us," Frank said authoritatively.

"It's been quite a while, you know."

"Yeah, I know, but only a day," he said, panning the sky. Noticing more water at his feet than just a few minutes ago, he grabbed one of the plastic cups retrieved from the plane and bent over and bailed water out of his area of the raft and passing it on to Yuto, motioning that he do the same and pass it on. "This will be an ongoing thing unless we can stop it," he said to Yuto.

The others also seemed to understand.

Feeling a bit refreshed, Frank stood carefully, inspecting the nooks and crannies of the raft hoping to find something new. The tip of a red strap peeked out under Otto. Kneeling down and crawling to him, Frank pointed down. Otto reacted and rolled to his left, and Frank pulled on the rubbery material attached to the strap. Whatever it was, it was huge and bright red.

"That's a cover for this raft. This will stop the water from soaking us, and if it rains, it sure will be a Godsend," Kimberly said softly while replacing the rag on her bloody head.

Frank wondered why she hadn't offered this information before. He guessed she was injured more than she or he suspected. She, indeed, was acting unusual.

That gash is pretty big. Did she suffer a concussion, too?

The cover was spread out, the edges lying on each passenger's lap. Each connection on the cover fit raised areas on the top of the sides of the raft, and the cover was soon being attached in an organized fashion. Once raised by two inflatable poles in the middle and to the sides, window flaps could be lowered to allow the breeze, if any, to ventilate the inside yet keep out the penetrating sun and exhausting heat. A silent celebration of sips from liter bottles of water followed.

Flares, a beacon, water, food, a flashlight, and now a cover. Christ, this is incredible. Kate would be proud that we found them. Now, I have to be sure we don't lose them. We really need food.

"What about food?" Otto asked.

A mind reader, now?

"There's a two-day supply of food rations in all rafts, uh, and, I think, saltwater desalting kits. I'm getting sort of goofy so let me think here. There is also a little, uh, fishing kit, I think. Yeah, there is. What else? Uh, a knife somewhere, and, geez, I can't seem to remember everything."

"We have some unused platters from last night's dinner, too—not many of them, mind you. Have to go slow with them just like the water," Frank said, considering the request spooky, especially right after he'd thought of food.

"I'm damn hungry. Break one of those suckers open now," Otto said, raising his voice.

Frank viewed the other's affirmation of Otto's request and opened two dinners. The food was devoured in no time. Frank reminded them not to drink too much water, but his pleas were being ignored, especially by Otto and Homer.

Better get found soon. The water and food will be gone shortly if these fools don't heed the warnings. Shit, the more that fat bastard drinks, the more the others will drink to keep up.

"Listen up, folks. I'm not kidding. I know you all think we are going to get rescued soon, but what if we were way off course, and they're searching elsewhere? We have to conserve food and water for the worst possible scenario."

No one seemed to hear his voice.

Finally, Helen spoke up. "Listen to the man, you assholes. Stop drinking all the fucking water and eating the food. Before you know it, we'll be destitute out here. Get real. We're survivors of a shitty crash. How often does that happen? Now, we need to rely on each other and get out of this shithole in one piece. Do you jerks want to live or die of stupidity?"

All eyes were upon Helen as she spoke about how cooperation must exist in this floating cosmos. Frank's pleas had been rejected, but the faces of the others showed understanding, reasoning, and concern.

Swearing at these idiots got their attention. I've told Kate this multiple times. She always scoffed at my justification for cussing. Wait until I tell her this one!

Cussing at times was a serious contention between Kate and Frank. Frank had been brought up with a bunch of boys in the neighborhood, and cursing was the way they made themselves feel like adults and all grown up. The more you cursed, the more the others thought of you as 'cool.' However,

Kate was not a fan of it. Her father did a lot of it, and it turned her off and embarrassed her for as long as she could remember. She loved her father, but his constant repetition of these words deflated his effect as a father figure in her eyes, and she didn't want that to happen to their children so she always showed some obvious disappointment when he cursed, often saying, "You don't want your little girl to grow up cussing, do you?"

But it was so difficult to stop cold turkey. It was as if the cursing was automatic, ingrained, so to speak. The words just blurted out without him thinking, often before he even knew he'd said them. He thought Helen's screaming and using the 'F' word proved his point. The people who weren't listening were shocked into listening for sure. Wasn't that a good thing?

"What's that in the water?" Irving said, pointing out of his portal in the cover.

Everyone leaned toward him, and the raft shifted, throwing several of them into the middle, crushing some of the dinners. Some continued to try to view what Irving had seen while others salvaged the food.

"Where?" Maxine asked.

"There," he said.

"Shit. It's a fin, a fucking shark's fin. He's going to attack. He's a Great White. Jesus Christ, get us out of here," shrieked Homer.

"Shut up, Homer. Stop making noise. It will only make him more suspicious. Sharks don't attack just to attack," said Irving.

"They do if they are hungry," Homer blurted.

"Contrary to your stupid beliefs, they don't, especially rafts and boats," Irving replied in a sarcastic tone.

"Yeah, I saw *Jaws*," Homer said with authority.

"That was Hollywood, not real life. Calm down. Keep quiet. Just watch the thing for now," Frank suggested.

For the next few hours, they remained fixated on the shark. It flowed through the water effortlessly while the front end searched and the back end guided the head to and fro. Its movements were repetitive and deliberate, and it certainly was not in a hurry and wasn't acting agitated. At times, it seemed the shark actually was looking up at the passengers and then glancing down as it turned. The gray leathery covering of its body was quite mesmerizing, and the dorsal fin was the central point, allowing them to follow it wherever it went. Occasionally, the shark dipped below the water, and the fin of the tail replaced it, but shortly after that, the dorsal fin reappeared and moved slowly passed the raft. There were other sharks nearby, but this one was the closest and for the longest time.

Then, it was gone. They were all gone. Rain in the form of a warm shower began. Frank and Yuto, with the help from Kimberly, fashioned the cover's top into a funnel to direct the rainwater into some empty bottles. Others scooped up any extra rainwater they could and drank it. It was considered a blessing from above, for sure. Otto seemed to be a dying animal trying to suck up and swallow any water near him. He couldn't use his right hand, but he licked his shirt and pulled it up to his lips with the left hand, all the while jerking his body around to lick the raft's edge where the raindrops were so obvious as they hit. Kimberly used a gentler technique, cupping her hands and sipping from the heels of them as water fell onto her fingertips. Others just leaned back with open mouths, and others placed their hands in a circle around their mouths as funnels.

~~ ~~ ~~

Maxine joyously kept licking her lips as the rain fell on her face and trickled down to her lips. She had her eyes closed, concentrating on something else rather than on the water getting to her mouth. In fact, she did not use her hands to direct the water at all. She was day dreaming back over her life, her childhood so poor but happy with six siblings—two brothers and four sisters—her love of music, and how exciting it was to be able to play the piano at their church, how the pastor had taken special steps to get her lessons for free, and the joy she got from teaching music and piano in her town's school in England.

She'd lost the love of her life relatively soon after being married and had never married again. The reality of life and how cruel it could be was exposed on that day. She was the matron of the small town. Everyone loved her, so she'd heard, and she gave back to the community much more than she ever received. This trip had been bought and paid for her to go to an international music conference in Argentina that she had been dreaming of for years. The town's people had all donated to a fund, unbeknownst to her at the time, and had presented it to her on her eighty-fifth birthday this year. Nothing could have been more unexpected than this gift, and she was humbled by it. She had kept her cancer and the treatments a secret from the town's people because she just knew how they would all react by showering her with food and other material things she didn't need. She couldn't let people sacrifice things for her for she felt she was on Earth to bring joy to others through her music.

~~ ~~ ~~

None of these castaways knew what pure rain water tasted like until now. How often, other than when a kid, did any of them just lean back and relax and drink from the sky as the rain fell? This water was like a pure mountain stream. It even had a tingling softness to it that tap water could never match. There was no smell to it, but each of them agreed there was a sensitivity, incredibly sweet, and a divine savoriness so wonderful that the receptors in their mouths could not taste anything more heavenly.

The rain didn't last long, but it did give hope.

Chapter Ten

The nights passed by slowly. Everyone slept for short periods, often being awoken by larger waves tilting the raft up and letting it flop back down onto the sea. The seawater then splashed onto their faces, despite the red roof and the attempts of many to cover their heads. The ever-present wind bursts spun the raft like a carousel off center, and as a result, the retching of a few roused the others.

The raft itself was yellow and square, approximately ten by twelve foot in size with sides that seemed to be a foot and a half to two feet high. There were two areas in the bottom for attaching the canopy with two pole-like structures so it stood up like a tent, and the sides of the canopy could be attached to hook-like devices on the raft's outsides. There was enough room so people could lean against the side and stretch their legs without getting in the way of one another once they figured how to position themselves. Yuto and Soo Mi were always clinging to each other, and Homer was always scrunched into an irregular ball with his thighs on his chest, resembling a fetal position. This gave plenty of room for the others to turn on their sides while they slept.

This day, the sun appeared on the horizon as a bright yellow-orange ball, a welcome sight from the dreary unknown of the night. Their thirst was soon temporarily quenched with the rainwater. Food was at a minimum, and it was clear everyone now understood the enormity of their situation. There wasn't going to be a quick recovery for them. They must have been so far off course that the rescue planes and ships were searching in the wrong areas, and as they drifted under the ocean's domination, the realization of truly being 'lost at sea' settled in. No one wanted to discuss their plight, probably through fear of panicking the others. They all had seen movies documenting plane crashes and how the searching of grids had taken days for the rescues.

The days wore on, leading to the uninvited nights. Each person, in their own way, counted the days but eventually realized that their computations were becoming more difficult as hours and nights passed without calculating them. Frank was the only one who knew. His watch was digital and set to display the date. Thirty-four days had gone by, but he thought it unwise to inform the others for fear of them becoming agitated and even more depressed.

Each day began with a precise count of water and food, allowing the passengers what they could drink and eat that day. The desalinating kits were of no use now. Prayers were persistently heard, urging God to be merciful upon them, water being the most important element mentioned. After consuming their one tiny rationed meal for the day, each person turned toward his own lookout post just by rolling onto their stomachs and propping themselves up on the side of the raft where they had slept.

Hours passed. Nothing was seen on the horizon nor in the sky. Conversations among the survivors was minimal. What was there to say?

"Hey, how's everyone doing?" Frank asked, breaking the prolonged silence. He had been thinking about what he was going to say because it just had to be said. He had heard that humans could go maybe three weeks without food.

Various moans and 'okays' came in response. A few people just stared at him, either in disbelief at the question, or they just didn't have the energy to answer.

"I know none of us want to hear or talk about this, but there will be a time that there is no food left. Hopefully, there will be rain for water, but no food," Frank stated as succinctly as possible.

"So what are you trying to say?" Maxine asked.

"Just that if we are going to survive, we need to have a plan," Frank answered.

"What do you suggest, man?" Homer asked, finally picking his head up from his knees.

"I don't know. I think we all need to think about it. That's all," Frank said.

There were no responses forthcoming. Silence enveloped the survivors.

Frank knew what plan was necessary. He didn't think anyone else would think of it, but he wanted to start them contemplating the possibilities in their minds, and when it was obvious that they couldn't develop one on their own, he would tell them his plan.

~~ ~~ ~~

Frank sighed. The wind mustered itself as it usually did this time of day, and, once again, the raft spun, a tin top out of control, slinging bodies around the raft like rag dolls, each person trying to right themselves against the weight of others. This was one of the most frustrating events on the raft because it sapped the strength of everyone, especially Maxine and Otto. In the beginning, the others had helped them because of their age and infirmity, but now, everyone was looking out for themselves. They were all suffering.

The wind is our great tormentor! It's blowing us southeast every day. I don't see us being rescued soon.

The gusts were increasing. The waves were higher, and the raft was being tossed more and more in every conceivable direction. They hung on in their own little nooks, grasping the rubber handles for dear life. Homer tried to steady Otto, but his size prohibited it. Otto's weight was crushing Homer at times. He had set his feet against the massive man to prevent Otto's uncontrollable rocking.

Frank steadied Maxine as well as he could, often looking down and seeing her once bright blue eyes fading to gray, exhibiting despair and physical weakness. A feeble smile from her parched lips appeared every once in a while, as if she thanked him for his care. He understood and smiled back.

Kate has blue eyes, the brightest blue I have ever seen. Are her eyes filled with tears now? I wonder how she's taking all of this. Is her family with her? Is she in contact with the airlines? How stressed out is she? How's the baby doing? Is it true stress may cause a miscarriage?

Visions of his wife crying while holding her abdomen that carried their first child clouded his senses. Despair was creeping in on him as well. How he dearly loved her but was blessed that she was not here. At least she and their child would live. Kate was stronger than she pretended, and he knew she would care for and nurture their child and be the best mother ever. He thought about his passing in the middle of this vast ocean and if she eventually would find someone else to love. This was not what he wanted to think of, but the thought continued to come into his head more than he wanted. Despair and loss of hope often placed more stress on one's mind than the physical loss of strength.

To clear his head, he watched Yuto and Soo Mi cling to each other, often wiggling into different positions but never letting go, her head snuggled into his neck and his chin over her eyes. Tears of hopelessness could not be distinguished from the saltwater splashing on her face, but they were there, together.

~~ ~~ ~~

Homer had curled himself into a ball, never changing position or shape. Some mentioned that they thought he had died or was dying, but an occasional deep breath and shivering of his body proved them wrong. His jacket was wrapped securely over his head, giving him some protection in the beginning but was now soaked with seawater.

He must have felt safe there—so safe he was afraid to change his posture. It was his safe space of life for now.

In his cocoon, Homer's mind was filled with anger, an anger that eclipsed the usual anger he had in his heart. His considered his life working in a fast food restaurant as useless. When growing up, he had been told he had such great potential. His parents had divorced; his mother left him to be raised by his dad who often told him that if he worked hard, success was right around the corner. His dad supported him in everything he did, encouraged him in every way, and tried to give him confidence in himself. His father's injury from a fall from a building on which he was laying bricks left him disabled and eventually destitute. His compensation payments were usually just enough to keep them going until they ran out. The compensation lawyer gave up on his case since there were questions about Homer's father's negligence being the cause of the fall, but his dad had always told Homer that wasn't so.

Somehow, everything that had happened was

just too much for his father, and he started drinking and became mean and detestable to his dying day. All of this was going on while Homer was growing up into his teens, and there was no family to support him. He was essentially on his own. Where was his potential, he asked himself? He had worked hard, and no success came. He knew his dad had to be right, but life never proved it to him. He just wanted to find his niche, something he could say he was good at. Flipping burgers for a living and going nowhere fueled the anger within him. He didn't care who he offended. He had been offended by his life, so why not make others as miserable as he?

~~ ~~ ~~

Helen and Kimberly had joined forces against the weather, covering themselves with parts of a tarp and hugging each other to keep comfortable. A short conversation could be heard from them every once in a while, but the contents were inaudible. They shifted positions many times an hour, assuming a spoon arrangement, then facing one another. They were following the directions that

Frank had told everyone: to move often, using their large muscles to create some heat while clinging to one another.

The mental and physical beating was becoming especially tough on Kimberly. She'd never had great stamina. She was brought up a spoiled child in a rich family but started to rebel against the forced authority of her parents. She'd flunked out of college and, just for spite, made a big deal about becoming a flight attendant. Surprisingly to her and those who knew her, Kimberly did very well and passed with flying colors. She really did find a job she actually enjoyed, and it kept her away from her family, so their constant bickering was no longer a bother in her life. She was never athletic, and her job, overall, did not require it, so she enjoyed life, and her social calendar was extensive when she wasn't working. She never had a beau or any guy interested in her because she could be a 'flake' at times and uninterested in any meaningful relationship. Her constant flighty demeanor away from her job had been a real turn off to many of her acquaintances, so they'd said, so she did not really have anyone she could call a friend.

Her only 'friend' was a roommate she had while sharing an apartment just before she'd gotten into the flight attendant program. Alice was an up-and-coming dancer/actress who Kimberly really liked. Their lifestyles were complimentary, and their work never caused them to compromise with each other. Then Alice had met Dave. Dave stole Alice's heart almost immediately. Kimberly has just gotten the gist of being a flight attendant, so Alice's love life wasn't any big deal to her; however, Kimberly's nuttiness and flirtatiousness infatuated Dave so much, he made advances toward Kimberly without Alice knowing. Kimberly told Dave, in no uncertain terms, that he was not her type. Actually, Kimberly didn't know what her type was. Dave continued his quest, and it soon became evident to Alice that Kimberly and Dave were 'a thing.' Instead of berating Dave, Alice verbally and once physically assaulted Kimberly for being a 'home-wrecker and a bitch.' Since that time, Kimberly had been turned off by anyone who got too close to her.

~~ ~~ ~~

The day was shortened by the dark overcast clouds, giving a sense of early nightfall. The relentless spinning of the raft had subsided, but the rocking carried on as the obstinate waves continued their onslaught to the sides of the raft. Night arrived, dampening the thoughts of rescue among the nine survivors once again.

Chapter Eleven

Hours led to more days of surviving. No one was counting the days anymore. Their world now was the raft, and the unknown was everywhere around them. Food was becoming the major problem for everyone. Each of them had tried their hand at using the fishing kit from the raft's supplies, but it had been unsuccessful with every attempt. Their frustration was almost palpable. Frank knew enough days had passed to make their situation desperate. The crew could barely move their arms and legs, and all were in a constant state of twilight sleep, unable to think clearly about almost anything. Delirium was just around the corner for some. It was obvious that the time for extreme measures was at hand if any of them were to live.

A heavy rain the night before had helped fill the bottles and containers with fresh water, but it was the meager amount of food left that none of the passengers wished to discuss for fear hunger would increase with just the mention of it. Floating in the ocean for days without any signs of land or aircraft was taking its toll slowly but surely. The incessant rocking of the raft had become accepted by all, each person moving in rhythm against the raft's motions. In contrast to their initial reactions of looking for hope in everyone's eyes, none of them now dared to gaze at the others, possibly afraid of seeing a deepening anguish in their faces.

"Well, Frank, what's the plan now, man? We ain't seen nothing, the food is good as gone. We just gonna fry in this pan?" Homer asked in a weak but angry voice. His facial expression was one of wide-eyed frustration.

"Food is the answer, folks," Frank finally said.

"You have a fishing line, Frank?" Homer asked as he appeared wide-eyed from his fetal position, pushing his coat from over his head.

"You okay, Homer?" Frank asked, surprised to see life in his companion.

Damn, how could he forget we all have failed at fishing?

"Yeah, I'm just alive. Just like all of us. Just alive. What food are you talking about?"

"Us," Frank said sternly.

"Jesus, you mean *us*, don't you? That's your fucking plan? You mean eating human flesh. Christ, you are some kind of sick dude," Otto blustered. "If I could, I would beat you to a pulp. That's my way of dealing with guys like you."

"As unpleasant and barbaric as it may seem, it may be our only choice in the weeks to come," Irving spoke in a matter-of-fact voice.

Frank thought that eating another human being was now filtering through the minds of each passenger. He had done it. He had awakened them to a grim excruciating reality. The mechanics of placing a piece of a person's muscle, uncooked, into one's mouth produced a repulsive response on each person's face as they clearly contemplated this physical action. It was even more sickening knowing that flesh was from someone they knew. They all then stared at Frank with disdain for thinking the unthinkable. He knew they had not thought past the taste of such a meal or how they would obtain it in the first place. He would just wait for someone to either question it or think of it on their own.

Living in the time of abundance and instant pleasure, Frank knew these people would never accept the idea of devouring one another's bodies, but he had succeeded in instilling the idea in their resistant minds. He would not harp on this vile action anymore until it was obvious that it was the only choice they had to live.

Is there a time period that must pass before we succumb to being animals, devouring whatever to stay alive? Our food is gone except for a few morsels, certainly not enough to feed us all. Am I too premature on this decision? This is just too much to think about.

The quiet stillness that ensued was surely commanding, each person obviously thinking more than ever about their lives, family, and loved ones. Soft crying from Soo Mi, Helen, and Kimberly broke the silence. The men stared at each other, now fully realizing the possibility of an inevitable confrontation with death. As if on cue, the flaps of the canopy were pushed back while they all searched the horizon and sky for any sign of help, an overt, last-ditch effort to cling to the hope of rescue and rid their minds of cannibalism. Nightfall was the only thing that pulled them from their search. All laid on their self-appointed sections of the raft with no visible expressions. Water bottles were being passed around, split lips sipping and mouthing the liquid as if solid food oozed from their containers.

Frank was trying his best to get comfortable by slowly wiggling around into a position appropriate for sleep. As he concentrated on his turn, he felt an odd lump underneath him. He lifted his body up so his elbows were on the side of the raft and his feet were on the bottom, but he saw nothing unusual underneath him. He relaxed again and turned in the same position with the side of his left leg on the raft. There, again, he felt a pressure on his leg. He searched under it and found nothing. As he brought his hand up his pants, he felt an object in one of the lower pockets of his cargo pants.

Oh my God, I never looked into Kate's surprise sac.

He reached into his pocket and retrieved the purple sac she had given him every time he traveled.

Turning so no one could see what he was doing, Frank gently opened the sac and emptied out five Hershey Kisses wrapped in silver with a white paper stuck to the side. He had forgotten the sac ever since the TSA guy had opened it. He smiled within himself and then devoured them quickly so the others would not beg for them. As he attempted to put the sac back, he felt something else in it. He then remembered, shook the sac upside down, and out flipped his nail clippers. Frank just had to chuckle a bit, wondering if Kate knew he had laughed during the most adverse time of his life because of her thoughtfulness. He slowly rubbed his fingers over the clippers, opened them up, and clipped a few nails, gently replaced them in the purple sac, and stuffed it back into his pocket.

Frank's mind wandered.

Kate, my love, please be by my side. Tell me what to do. I miss you so. Will these people understand the dire situation we will soon be in? The sun is so hot. The night is so cold. Oh, Kate, please come to me. I love you so. Will I ever see you again?

Frank's dream that night was a strange one for him. He dreamt he and Kate were on vacation on some beach, staring out into an ocean, pointing out dolphins and surfers in the waves. They laughed and hugged one another and then repeated the same actions over and over. It was almost comical as, in the dream, the laughing got louder and louder, often drowning out any of their conversations. Suddenly, Kate was gone, and Frank turned to search for her, spotting a young child walking away from the beach umbrella that he and Kate had erected. Kate was nowhere to be found, and yet he could hear her laughing as he called out her name. He found himself in the surf searching for her when a voice behind him yelled something inaudible, causing him to swivel and be swamped by a large wave knocking him under the water so hard he could not right himself. The voice became more audible, and he fought to get to the surface.

His eyes finally popped open, and he took a deep breath, trying to focus on what was staring him in the face.

"Hey, Mr. Cannibal, what's your plan now?"

Homer asked, leaning over Frank face to face.

Jesus. Where's Kate? Oh, God, a bad dream, and now this jerk! It hasn't dawned on him yet.

Frank could only gaze into Homer's despondent eyes, shrug, and spread his hands. The answer was in his physical response.

"How and when?" Irving asked.

"Draw straws, I guess?" Frank said. "We all will decide when."

Then Frank withdrew from the rest, pulling his makeshift covers over his head, trying desperately to find Kate in his dream.

Chapter Twelve

A soft breeze blew all night. Intermittent rain helped the thirst once again. The cadenced rocking of the vessel continued. So far as Frank could tell, everyone but him was asleep. As the sun began to light up the eastern sky, Frank sat up by pushing on the bottom of the raft. His hands slid in a gooey slime of fluid, and he fell back. There wasn't enough light to see what the substance was. He squinted against the sun's reflective rays. His heartbeat quickened as he saw the color of the fluid. It was a reddish maroon and very sticky.

Almost like fresh clotted blood.

"Jesus, it is blood," he said softly.

He looked around the raft, starting at the other end. No source could be found. As he turned to his left, Maxine was lying still, supine, and with a gray, pasty appearance. A hooked knife and its loose sheath was on her belly, and both wrists had been sliced open. Beside her laid a placard listing an inventory of the raft equipment.

"Shit, Maxine committed suicide," he yelled.

Only a few people reacted with moans.

"Goddamn it, people, Maxine committed suicide," Frank spoke louder to wake everyone.

The women gasped at the sight of Maxine's lifeless body, and Helen screamed at the pool of blood she laid in. The men could only stare in disbelief.

"Why? Why did she do it?" Helen's voice cracked.

"She couldn't handle it anymore," Otto said. "I know how she feels, uh, I mean, felt."

"Do you think she did it for us knowing she would be the first to go?" Soo Mi asked.

"Possibly, but we'll never know," Frank answered.

Helen's voice broke in. "She told me she had cancer. Her pills were lost in the crash. I guess she knew she was going to die from the cancer or possibly felt all was lost, so why not? She seemed to be the kind of person who thought of others before herself. I think she did it for us," said Helen.

"Cancer? Jesus." Homer growled.

"Where did knife come?" Yuto asked in broken English. He reached over her body and turned her to reveal a red case with a large white 'plus' sign on it.

Kimberly gasped, "Oh, my God, it's the kit for emergencies. Damn! That's the knife I told you about. And there, there, the list of stuff on the raft. I'm forgetting a lot. I can't remember anything they taught me. This is not supposed to be happening to me," she said and broke out crying.

"For God's sake, how we bury?" Yuto asked.

"Yeah, Mr. Cannibal, how do we?" Homer barked at Frank.

"I think we pray for her first," Frank answered, specifically gazing at each passenger before he stared intently at Homer. He bowed his head in silent prayer as the others slowly closed their eyes and bent their heads. No one spoke a word, even after lifting their heads.

Now they know what is next. None of them want to say it.

An indeterminable period of time passed while they pondered their destiny. Their thoughts were probably all the same, but no one could look at anyone else but Frank. He had been the creator of the plan. He should do something. Frank felt their visual contact without raising his head.

Jesus, what would Kate do? What should I do? Do I become a barbarian right in front of these people?

The answer became apparent with Irving sliding to his right, looking around at everyone, grasping the knife off Maxine's stomach, and beginning to cut her clothes off. None of the other survivors moved. No one offered to help or tried to stop him. Her left leg was now naked from her panties down. Irving's hands shook as the tip of the blade was lowered through her wrinkled skin. Dark, semi-coagulated blood slowly oozed around the chrome blade. The motion was almost surgical, not too deep and carried straight to the lower thigh just above the knee without cutting the muscular tissue. He then cut the top portion of skin in a 'T' and the lower part of the incision into an inverted 'T', splaying the skin first to his right and finally to his left to expose the muscles of her thigh. Using his fingers, he separated the rest of the skin and the small layer of fat from the muscle.

Hands were placed over mouths, and some forced their fingers over their eyes. Gasps of disbelief were uttered with each motion of the knife. As they did, they also slid as far away from Irving as they could, as if trying to escape the inevitable. Homer vomited bile over the side of the boat. Then Otto belched as if to do the same but didn't.

As Irving skillfully separated the muscle groups by their fascial linings, he must have felt the group's overwhelming sickening response behind him.

Irving looked over his shoulder and turned to the rest. "Hey, I used to hunt deer when I was a kid."

Each passenger mumbled that they felt Maxine had offered herself as her last gift of joy to eight people she never really knew, and now, she was to be consumed by them for nourishment.

And so it had come to pass. They all finally understood their fates.

Chapter Thirteen

Quietude hovered over the eight remaining souls on board their life raft. Clotted blood about their mouths was evident, even after saline washes were used to clean away the evidence of savagery. Frank felt that each of the passengers had become more distant from one another, even though they were physically close. It could be seen even in the eyes and gestures of Yuto and Soo Mi. What had they done? They had actually devoured a fellow survivor, a human like themselves. What would people think? This was undoubtedly on the minds of the lost crew. Hunger had been temporarily remedied, but their actions leading to this would never be justified in their minds. And the most pressing question of all? Am I next—and when?

Life is so precious. Maxine knew that. In death, she knew how cherished life is. May God have mercy on her soul. Kate, you would have loved her.

~~ ~~ ~~

The waves became higher and heavier as the day hours droned on. The wind was swirling and rotating the craft in irregular circles once again. Bailing water was the duty of the day if they were to prevent the sea from drowning them. In actuality, the bailing did take their minds off Maxine's fate. The weeks so far of mechanically staying alive had taught them all what was expected of each without a word being said. Frank occasionally gave positive feedback to those who worked especially hard. He knew it helped that person to stay focused as well as letting others know what was expected of them. As his superiors had witnessed with his people skills back at the firm, he did indeed excel at this.

Maxine's body was kept covered so as not to gross out everyone during the non-eating times as well as to keep it from decomposing faster in the sun and the wind. Frank, aided by Irving, had told everyone that her meat had to be eaten as quickly as possible, leaving the heart, kidneys, and liver until the end. The 'food' was only good for a short period of time. Maxine soon became 'that over there.' Continuing to use her name was unnerving to all.

~~ ~~ ~~

Otto was the least helpful of all. Sure, his broken arm was a physical handicap, but his large frame and immobility was sapping the strength of the rest. While asleep, his massive body often slid into the middle of their craft, making it difficult to get anything done and cramping the rest of the passengers' spaces. Frank and the others knew he would never volunteer to perform any act of heroism as Maxine had done. No one would say it, but they could only wish for him to select the short straw at the first drawing.

I wish Otto could leave us somehow. My God, Kate, what should I do? What can we do?

~~ ~~ ~~

Otto stared at his misshapen right arm. He often moved his fingers, but the pain was just so much, but, as the days had turned to a week or more, the pain remarkably became less and, at times, gone. He wondered if he had gangrene, but he always thought the fingers would turn black and fall off with that disease process, and his fingers were the same color as his left hand. He thought about whether there was a time limit on getting his arm set and healed. Did the doctors have to get to him in a certain time to fix it, or would they just shake their heads and tell him it was inoperable? He didn't know much about bones. What would a bar owner know about bones? Sure, many a bone was broken when he was in charge and in fights in his bar over the years, but the emergency people always picked these folks up and took them to the hospital. He never knew what happened to them or if their bones ever healed. He then thought of his kids. They were all grown up, but would any of them take over the bar or would they just sell it? After his divorce, he hadn't had much to do with them. He'd left it equally to all of them, three of them, to do whatever they wanted.

So much for a legacy.

~~ ~~ ~~

"Over there! I see something. It's a boat. I see a boat!" Kimberly screamed, pointing to the empty sea ahead of her.

"Where? Where is it?" Yuto asked, turning his head back and forth, trying to see where the vessel was.

"There. There. Can't you see it?"

"I'm not sure," Yuto's voice dropped. "Are you sure you see something?"

"Goddamn it. I'm not crazy. Look, there," Kimberly said with a distinct crackling voice coming from between dried lips.

Everyone was now searching the horizon for Kimberly's boat, heads darting to and fro, but no one saw anything. The vigil continued for five to ten minutes, and eventually all eyes fell on Kimberly, some pitiful and others angry. Frank's and Helen's eyes met, them silently questioning whether Kimberly had actually seen something or had imagined the whole thing. Their conclusion was unanimous. Yuto, Soo Mi, and Irving returned to their chores before the commotion. Otto fell asleep, and Homer continued to search, trying desperately to pinpoint the boat Kimberly was still pointing out, although silently now.

"It's gone. Jesus, it's gone," she said as tears burst from her eyes and loud, uncontrolled sobbing followed.

Soo Mi placed her arm around her, rocking back and forth to calm her.

"We should have shot off a flare," Kimberly kept saying.

The sighting was never mentioned again. Time continued to pass almost unnoticed now. The days were taking their toll upon them.

Chapter Fourteen

The sound was horrendous. An upheaval of painful belching combined with guttural explosions was soon followed by Otto sitting up grabbing his chest, nostrils flaring, eyes bulging in disbelief, and small blue veins appearing on his red cheeks. He reached for the side of the raft, trying to lean over the side to vomit. He then collapsed in a twisted bulbous mass, slumped over the raft's edge. His body slowly slid back into the center of the raft, drawn by its sheer size.

Frank stared in shock.

My God! He's had a heart attack. He's dead. This is so freaky.

"What happened?" Helen asked, her teeth clattering from fright.

"I think he just die heart tack," Yuto answered.

Irving leaned over the body, trying to ascertain any breathing from the massive hulk. With his ear to Otto's mouth, he felt for a pulse in the left wrist. The gradual blue hue of death became evident over

Otto's face and lips as Irving desperately attempted to find some sign of life. He finally looked up at everyone, shook his head, and flopped back to his place on the boat.

Time continued to pass slowly for all. It was impossible not to stare at the remains of their large comrade.

"Well, at least we don't have to draw straws yet," Homer said nonchalantly from underneath the cover over his head.

As if on automatic, all heads turned, and the survivors gazed intently at Homer's body with disgust.

"Jesus, let's be real. We're here in a shitty situation. His death is a blessing for us. There's a lot to eat," Homer continued on from his hiding place.

Now that statement hit deep into everyone's psyche. The reality of it all is now settling in. Look at their faces. Christ, this is so bad, Kate, I miss you so much; I love you.

Homer's words lingered over the rest of them for a long time, each clearly contemplating the actual truth in them. Finally, Irving looked at Frank and Yuto and then at Maxine's body. Not a word was spoken as the men moved to wrap her fleshless corpse in the tarp, slowly and reverently placing her on the side of the raft and bowing their heads in silent prayer before letting her body slide into the sea from the tarp. At first, she floated next to the raft as if she didn't want to leave. She then separated from them and slowly submerged into its massive underwater grave. Frank rinsed and then folded the tarp while everyone watched Maxine disappear.

Irving let some time pass by before speaking. He leaned over, picked up the knife, and said, "Homer was right on one thing. We don't have to draw straws." He waited for any responses. None were forthcoming. "While we're on the subject, I will, at some time, draw the short straw, and it could be the next time, so everyone here will need to know how to use this knife. I know it is sickening to many of you, but our situation demands not standing on ceremony. You need to watch and learn how to do this."

As he looked around at each member, the

responses to this ultimatum compelled Irving to add, "You have to learn to do this, damn it. There is absolutely no other option here."

Look at these people. They are at their wit's end. Thank God for Irving's perseverance!

Irving started with Otto's left leg just as he had with Maxine, but this time, the maroon texture of muscle did not appear. Instead, large yellow blobs oozed from underneath the knife and gradually billowed over the skin. He had to use an old rag and some of Maxine's clothes to hold the slippery, fatty tissue back so he could continue cutting down to muscle. This entailed a much larger 'T' above and below Otto's thigh.

Soo Mi suddenly gasped, choked, and turned to the ocean and vomited. This unfortunately caused Kimberly to follow suit, and finally Homer, trying desperately not to look at the body as if he couldn't stand it any longer. He heaved his chest on the opposite side of the raft and eliminated his stomach contents. None of the three turned around for a long time.

The dissection took much longer than Frank

expected because of the enormity of the individual Irving was cutting apart. The skin and blubber attached to it slid back and forth on the wet floor of the raft. It certainly was not a sight some could bear to witness. Unfortunately, Irving could not just throw the fat overboard for fear of the sharks returning.

Irving, focusing only on delivering the meat to his comrades, did not seem to realize the disgusting and barbaric condition he had exposed until he had stopped for a breather. He turned and witnessed the sullen faces that had been watching his actions, and then he must have known. To his credit, he also must have realized that he was keeping folks alive.

Fortunately for us, Irving is here to feed us. No one else here could have done this, including me. This ain't crab cakes, Kate. My God, where am I?

Chapter Fifteen

The intermittent rains continued, always giving the survivors enough fresh water to quench their thirst and keep bodily functions from shutting down. By now, modesty had fallen by the wayside. Men urinated and defecated over the side, clearly not feeling the urge to hide anything. Women squatted and filled plastic bags, emptying then reusing them. They used small sections of Maxine's and Otto's clothes to wipe themselves after moving their bowels. No one seemed to care who saw what. In the back of their minds, they must have felt they were all either going to die or, if rescued, never attempt to see each other again, so it didn't matter.

Otto's flesh tasted differently than Maxine's, but there was plenty of it. Realizing this, some of the survivors ate more with binging episodes followed by long periods of sleep. The major pig was Homer, a man, Frank suspected, destined to be the first to become unhinged emotionally. Kimberly was the next. She was almost psychologically and physically drawn to copy Homer's actions to a lesser degree but more than the rest.

Could this binging and bloating be good for them? Should I be doing this? Kate, I'm so glad you're not here.

Homer acted more and more like a dog who ate everything placed in front of him. He ate until he no longer had the strength to move. Granted, Otto presented a smorgasbord of sustenance, but Homer and Kimberly clearly did not realize that this, too, would be gone soon, and others taking their place would offer less. The gorging would have to stop. Even Soo Mi and Yuto began to act in a similar manner, obviously driven by the repetitive actions of the other cannibals. At times, hyenas could be daintier about their eating habits.

"Psst," Frank whispered into Irving's ear.

The rest had finished attacking the mass of meat in front of them.

"What?" Irving replied, rubbing his salt-crusted eyes.

"We can't let these people binge like this. What happens when there's no more Otto? His size makes them think the food is never going to run out."

"Yeah, I was thinking the same thing. What are you proposing, Frank?"

Frank gazed down at the maroon-encrusted knife lying by Irving's side. "You get the knife. We are going to have to protect the food source, man. If they don't abide by reason, we'll have to be forceful," Frank insisted.

"Shit. So it's come to this. Fighting among ourselves," Irving said.

"Hey, we didn't start the binge crap, you know. That idiot hippy over there went bullshit, and Kimberly and Soo Mi are being sucked into it," Frank explained.

"I know, I know. Okay, we start tomorrow morning, telling them that we will have to ration the food, that binging is not a successful way for all of us to survive. They have to understand," Irving said with a fixed stare into Frank's eyes.

"And if dope-ass doesn't understand?" Frank asked.

Irving shrugged, threw his hands up, and rolled over to sleep.

~~ ~~ ~~

Homer woke first, stretching toward the sky, yawning and reaching for one of the bottles of water. He chugged the precious fluid in one enormous sloppy gulp after another, and, before putting the bottle down, he eyed the monstrous flesh before him. His face changed from contentment to absolute frustration as he searched for the knife to break his brief fast. It was nowhere to be found. He crawled aimlessly over the others, pushing objects aside and peering under the slowly awakening passengers' legs and arms for the chrome blade.

"Where's the fucking knife, you bastards?" Homer shouted. He was on his knees threatening each person, pivoting around in the center of the craft. "You take it, shithead?" he yelled at Frank. "No, you, you piece of shit," he confronted Yuto.

Suddenly, Homer was flat on his back bleeding from the side of his head and partially unconscious. Standing above him was Helen.

"I've had enough of your pigging out and

mouthing off. We all have had it. I have the knife," she said, holding an iron bar that she'd gotten from God knew where in her hand. "We are all going to listen to Frank and Irving from now on. No one is going to run this fucking show on his own and do whatever he wants. We are all in this together. Do you hear me?" she said, standing above him and screaming each word independently into Homer's ear.

Homer groaned and nodded in the affirmative and pressed a rag to his swollen head. Frank and Irving looked at each other in amazement and smiled. Helen reached across Homer with the knife in her fist as if to stab him but passed by him and gave the knife to Irving. Homer winced as she moved back over him, truly believing she was going to cut him to pieces.

Now that is what I've been waiting for. That is what Kate would have done. No swearing, of course. Good job, Helen.

Chapter Sixteen

Frank twitched quickly awake as he heard, "Frank, you sleeping?" He rubbed his eyes to get the sleepiness from them and again heard, "Wake up, you sleepyhead." It was Kate, standing over him brushing her teeth with one hand and twirling her hair with the other. "We're going to miss the concert tonight if you can't get your butt out of bed, now!"

"What concert?" he replied.

"Oh my gosh, have you gone daft? The Marble Heads, dopey."

The Marble Heads had been Frank's favorite band for years before he'd met Kate, and he had been trying all this time to get her to go to one of their concerts. She had heard them once and hadn't been impressed, but she loved Frank so dearly that she'd said she felt it was her duty to go and pretend how 'wonderful' they were. She rubbed his head quickly back and forth to arouse his still, sleepy demeanor and then sat on the edge of the bed massaging his neck and shoulders.

Her massage felt invigorating, and he wished it would never stop.

"What time is it?" he asked.

"Five-thirty, and the concert is at eight. You keep on lying in bed with your eyes slammed shut, we will never even have time to eat before it starts."

Kate's hands were like a professional masseuse, gently but rhythmically kneading his skin and superficial muscles. Her actions were intended to fully wake him, but, in fact, seemed to put him more at ease than rouse him. He loved this about her. It was one of the things that captivated him. She had this aura around her in just about everything she did, especially when it involved her touching him. Her soft warm breath on his face and neck increased his awareness of her and relaxed him even more. What she was doing now was not a sexual thing. When making love, her touch was much more arousing and at times sinful. This gentle, soothing, waxing and waning motion of her hands was meant to reassure him, cajole him, and keep him closer to her.

She made his entire body now feel as if it were

floating on air. Soon, her soft breaths increased across his face and became stronger, and her fingers seemed to tighten into a firm grasp rather than how they'd been minutes before. It got to a point that she was actually hurting him with her forceful deep plunging hands, all of which caused his eyes to suddenly pop open to divulge a foggy, blurred vision of a woman over him.

"Frank?" Helen asked. "Frank, wake up. That can't be comfortable the way your neck is smashed up against that rubber handle and your face being pelted by the wind. Roll over."

Frank shook his head to wake up and get a hold of himself as he reentered his world of hopelessness.

"Uh, thanks, it was getting to be unbearable. You were right."

More unbearable than you'll ever know.

Chapter Seventeen

After what seemed an eternity, there wasn't much flesh left to eat on Otto's corpse. They all said they felt like those ugly vultures picking at a skeleton of a deer on the side of a road. Only small pieces were left, hardly enough to eat, but there they were, and the crew couldn't help themselves. No knife was needed to get to the loose carrion hanging off the thigh, leg, and ankle areas. What was most disturbing to all was the actual sight of the two broken bones in what was once Otto's right arm, but the appearance of them did not deter them from obtaining any bit of food to eat.

Finally, they all decided what they had to do. Frank suggested that they rid themselves of Otto's body but only when there was a hard wind that blew the raft around and caused it to float it a good distance from where they would drop the body. That way, they wouldn't have to worry about the sharks upsetting the raft to get to them.

That day came. The wind picked up, and

everyone muttered their relief that it had started. Interestingly enough, they'd all said they feared the wind, but now it was welcomed. As the raft increased in speed, it spun and blew every which way. Frank and Irving quickly dumped Otto into the waves. He disappeared in a blink of an eye. That was that.

Who was going to be next? Straws would have to be drawn soon, and they all knew it. No one spoke. No one looked at anyone. They were all alone, not only in the raft on an unforgiving sea, but alone in themselves for now. Days had passed since their last food intake.

~~ ~~ ~~

The slap in the face was not a welcoming feeling. Another slap on Frank's leg was annoying, and the next one on his chest was infuriating. Despite his weakened condition, he bolted upright with his fist cocked and his right arm back behind his head ready to impart a mighty blow to whomever was hitting him. Once his eyes popped open, he leaned forward to get better leverage—and saw nothing.

The rest of the crew were sleeping and evidently much more in a weakened state than him. And then he saw the culprit, and joy screamed out of his mouth for the first time since the crash. "Holy God has answered us! Wake up, it's feast time!"

Below him, flopping on the bottom of the raft, were three weird-looking fish with two large dorsal fins flailing about. The others stretched out from their nightly cocoons of misery and clearly weren't privy to his scream of happiness until they, too, saw the fish. Helen grabbed the knife from the sock of a still-sleeping Irving and was about to stab each fish to kill them when Frank yelled, "No! If you miss, you'll puncture the raft. Be cool." He reached down to retrieve a piece of clothing, grabbed a fish, took the knife from her, and cut its head off.

He proceeded to do the same for the other ones when suddenly two more fish landed in the raft. The crew went crazy trying to catch them, to the point it became a game to corner them and give them to

Frank.

Finally, there was some levity amongst the passengers as well as a camaraderie that had not been present since after Maxine and Otto had died. Frank handed the knife and then one fish one at a time to Irving, who gladly cleaned them. Nothing could have been more satisfying to the crew than the raw fish, something they would have never eaten had it been placed on their plates for dinner at home, but, being famished and so thoroughly hungry for anything other than human flesh, this made the raw, bloody fish taste like a delicacy.

As they ate, their lessons of the weeks at sea of never overindulging or binging was evident. Each ate tiny morsels of the flying fish that had been so kind to drop into their world of misery. They all took time to relish each bite and even waited after swallowing for a moment to savor the overall joy of fresh protein. Each one looked at the other, eyes met eyes, heads nodded in happiness, and they ate.

"So, we have feast of good fortune," said Yuto. "We need thank God for our blessing." He lowered his head and brought both hands up as if cradling an invisible gift and spoke as the others followed his lead. "Dear God, our heavenly Lord, we thank you for holy gift, gift that hopefully will help until you find right time see others find us. We were lost, but now you find us, and we here so grateful. In name your holy son, Jesus of Nazareth, thank you again. Amen."

Mumbled 'amens' followed. All looked at each other, and smiles again appeared on everyone's faces. These grins broke into raucous laughter after two more flying fish fell into the boat. Even Homer became lively and animated, expressing bliss that the others felt but a joy he said he had never known in his life.

No one had qualms about keeping some of the fish for a little later, so Irving did not clean them right away in an attempt to keep them fresh. He wrapped them in a canvas and tied a rope around it so they were safe from falling out and then stashed them away. No one seemed to feel anything but pride in their accomplishments at that moment.

More fish flew in the boat over the next few hours. No ceremony was necessary. Each fish caught was killed and wrapped with the others. The amount of these kamikaze fish was enough to keep their hunger satisfied for several more days and possibly for more than that if they were cautious. A calm came over the group. Everyone was silent, seemingly satiated and pleased at their victory.

Homer sat up a few hours later, and in a soft, discerning voice—not his usual snarling tone—said, "You know, I never was a good fisherman; in fact, my dad said, when it came to fishing, I was the 'kiss of death.' He always had great success fishing. He loved it. He would go anytime he could, but when I went with him something always happened, and he caught very few, if any fish. One time, he ended up accidentally throwing his new rod into the water when casting, another time the engine caught on fire, and the one time he did catch one, I knocked off the line with the net trying to bring it into the boat. But, Goddamn it, he would have been proud of me today."

Homer then turned, laid down, and repositioned himself into a ball and pulled his covers over himself.

Quizzical looks appeared on the passengers' faces, each turning to see the other's reaction. A tiny smile appeared on everyone's mouths, followed by a collective sigh.

Chapter Eighteen

With their bellies satisfied, the crew independently seemed to drift off into a safe and secure space, some just gazing at the sky and maybe envisioning some pleasant images. Homer seemed to have become mired in a trance as he had turned on his side and was staring at the bloody carcasses of the fish they had just eaten. His demeanor was not one of hunger or contentment but seemingly a disdain for the dead creatures below him. His eyes looked as though he was intently angry. Suddenly he snatched a fish up and threw it overboard, unbeknownst to the rest of his compatriots. Then again, he reached and snatched up another bloody body and flipped it over the side.

This time, Helen saw it and nudged Frank, silently notifying him of Homer's actions, even though Frank had witnessed it for himself. Frank swung around as Homer threw a third fish overboard, and screamed, "Hey, what the hell are you doing? You're throwing away our food, and those are bloody, damn it. Blood can be smelled for miles underwater by sharks. Stop it before we are inundated by them!"

Homer turned and stared at Frank as if he were an alien being. It was as if he could not detect or understand anything Frank was saying. Then he straightened up and responded in an unfamiliar, slow and calm tone of voice, "Yes...sir! Captain...Cannibal! I will...cease...and...desist. At...your...service, Captain." He sluggishly turned away, sat, and pulled an old rag over his head.

Silence reigned on the raft. No one said a thing, but Frank's alarming words were clearly understood by the rest, and they all looked over the sides for anything swimming nearby.

It didn't take long, and Soo Mi pointed out to sea. She kept pointing, but no one except Frank seemed to see her. She was speechless for a time and then said, "There! They're here!"

Everyone directed their attention to her side of the raft and followed her finger out to a point where two fins were identified swimming toward them. Homer never moved from underneath his cover.

"Okay, folks, let's be cool. Get down as close as possible to the floor of the raft and don't move, and above all, do not talk. We don't want them to get any inkling there is dinner aboard this table," Irving whispered.

They all did what he suggested. Only Frank and Irving kept their heads up just enough to keep tabs on the sharks.

The two fins became five fins in the blink of an eye. Frank thought better of telling the crew this fact. In their usual manner, the sharks circled out farther away from the boat and kept their distance as if to purposely check out this unknown beast floating in their waters that was related to blood and a possible delicious meal. The circling came closer, so close Frank could have touched one of their fins as it drifted past the side of the raft. Then another and another came by.

As he watched, suddenly on the other side, the raft lifted up a bit then flopped back into the water. A shark had tested the beast. Kimberly almost choked on her attempt to not scream. A slight murmur of air being sucked into her frightened body could be heard. Frank looked over to her and gave her the okay sign with his thumb and index finger. Kimberly blinked her bulging eyes in response, but it was evident that she may not be able to control herself.

Then again, on Frank's side, a shark lifted the raft. This time it was much higher, and when it finally let loose, the noise of the raft hitting the water was like a giant wave slapping against a rock. More guttural sounds came from Kimberly, Soo Mi, Homer, and then Helen. They tried their best to keep quiet, but it was becoming obvious the sharks were not just going to leave them alone like the last encounter.

At last, the raft remained relatively silent in the water. Frank peeked over the side in every direction, rapidly shifting his eyes from right to left and back. He nudged Irving to do the same on his side. Irving reported back by signing him with his hands.

"None seen," Irving said.

Frank whispered, "Me neither."

They both waited for a minute or so.

Nothing.

"They may have gone," Frank said in a louder whisper.

Everyone stared at Frank as if they could not understand.

He repeated, "They may have gone. Be quiet and very still. Don't move at all until we're sure."

There was an enormous, collective sigh of relief when they all seemed to relieve their bodies of the stress as they became more loose and relaxed.

With one gigantic rush of seawater over the side of the raft, a shark rammed the vessel, lifting it almost two to three feet. Screams and gasps could no longer be kept internalized. They were grabbing on to anything that seemed stable enough to prevent them from being propelled from their home. Bodies were being thrown around the floor of the raft, ricocheting off one another. And then another attack ninety degrees from the original hit, sending more bodies now elevated off the floor to land on each other.

"Everyone, lie flat down on the bottom of the raft to steady it, now!" Irving barked.

Every passenger did as they were told except Homer, who had stayed so still with a shirt over his head during it all. He finally reacted, threw off the covering, and screamed in a raspy, growling voice, "Face it, you bastards, we're all going to die now. No one's going to help us." He stood teetering on his spindly legs set between the passengers on the bottom of the raft and stared aimlessly at everyone, eyes psychotically wide open.

Then another enormous attack broadside lifted the raft again. Homer screamed, flipped up and over the side, and was gone.

Frank and Irving were the first to notice. They innately searched the boat first and then the nearby ocean water. "Homer's overboard. Anyone see him?" Frank asked.

All eyes aboard scanned around the raft, finally settling on an area of extreme bubbling and thrashing of fins and fleeting glimpses of shark bodies. In the middle of it welled up a mass of bright red blood, a lower leg and foot connected to a green sneaker. The spectacle continued to mesmerize the crew for two to three minutes of horror.

And then another silence—a silence that lasted for a long time until Kimberly spoke with a fearful, vibrating voice, "They're gone, right? They...they got their meal, right? Right?"

Frank responded quickly, "It's been ten or so minutes. I would have thought they would have been back sooner if they were to continue their barrage. Yes, I think they're gone. Jesus, what the hell did he think he was doing?"

Yuto said, "He not thinking."

He wasn't thinking, all right. Homer had hit the wall. Everyone in this kind of situation does eventually, I guess. Hopefully, we will not have this happen again. If so, a lot more walls will be hit.

Chapter Nineteen

The next few days were uneventful. A routine had set in. The men separated from the women, the men on one side of the raft and the women on the other. It just happened that way. No one suggested it. It was a natural thing to happen in this type of grave situation. Even Yuto and Soo Mi had done so. Before, they were performing their duties without privacy, but with some food in their bodies, they had obviously begun to think more clearly and were now trying to return to being more civil. Each man took his turn eliminating himself as the others tried to block the view from the ladies and vice versa. Overall, it was silly to think complete privacy existed, but humans did have some innate sense of it even when conditions didn't warrant it.

Some seemed to be responsible for 'house' cleaning chores while others remained vigil and stared out over the ocean for any signs of rescue. Every activity was exhausting, and a sleeping period for some appeared random, while the others maintained an inward clock that decided their sleeping habits. Those who slept seemed to wake on cue, allowing the others to slip off into their dreamlands. And so these routines rolled on just as the raft rolled to and fro, rocking its inhabitants gently. No one knew how long they had been lost except Frank, and he wasn't going to remind them.

Usually, Yuto and Soo Mi tried to sleep and work together. It was obvious they were so in love, and it was this love that was keeping them sane. Helen and Kimberly were once a pair in everything they did, but recently, Kimberly had drifted away from everyone. Frank and Irving talked shop and discussed means of survival, but that was about it for their relationship.

One afternoon, Helen rose onto her knees and said, "We all have been together for a long time on this raft. I think we are all drifting away from one another into our own worlds, and I'm not sure this is a good thing. We have nothing to do on this godforsaken raft, so don't you think we should start conversing with one another to keep our minds sharp and not focusing on our destiny?"

Soo Mi replied, "What should we do?"

"Let's tell each other about ourselves from birth on. Tell us what you have done, what you will do, and what you want to do. Anything to keep us interested in something. It's bound to get us talking and asking questions, conversing, don't you think?" Helen said.

Everyone looked at each other, waiting for someone to answer 'yea' or 'nay.'

Frank spoke up, "It certainly is better than wallowing in our own misery."

"I'm in," said Irving.

Then the rest shook their heads in agreement.

"I guess you the leader," said Soo Mi to Helen.

"Okay, here goes. I was born in Intercourse, Pennsylvania." Everyone started to snicker, and Helen broke into a laugh. "Well, I have never told anyone this until now, so I guess it was the best time to do it. I didn't think I'd get that reception."

The others continued to laugh and smile a bit.

I gotta admit it was funny to hear that word out here in the middle of nowhere.

"Anyway, I guess I had a normal childhood. Two

brothers, one sister. She died falling from a tree house my dad had built. It wasn't his fault. Annie was doing something stupid. Dad had put a lot of safety things around for us and taught us what to do and what not to do, but he never lived her death down. It haunted him forever. Mom brought us up and never did mention Annie. It was as if she'd never existed, and I guess that helped Mom through it all.

"I went away to college after high school. Never did come home much. Yeah, Christmas, I did, and on Thanksgiving a few times. Married this guy Rick, from Argentina. Met him at a party in a hair salon, dated him for a while, and we eloped my senior year. No kids." She hesitated. "Yeah, no kids!

"Rick did his own thing, you know, but his mother got sick, and he moved her from Argentina to live with us. That was the beginning of the end of my life, I guess. Maria was so demanding, and Rick did everything she wanted, and then he expected me to do the same. I thought she was complaining just to get him to be with her and not me. I resented it. I went out on my own and opened up a flower shop. I had to. I just had to get away from her. Got pretty good at it, too. Made money, the shop grew."

Helen shivered, and tears rolled from her eyes. She sniffled and wiped her nose and eyes with her wrinkled blouse. "Anyway, Rick soon hated me for resenting her, and you know that didn't go well, that's for sure. We'd scream and yell and then not speak for days, and all this time this woman was getting sicker and sicker, and I didn't think she was sick. But she was. I'm so sorry I was a fool. I was into myself and nothing else, I guess. I had no Rick, no family of my own, and I guess I felt sorry for myself."

Helen looked out over the ocean for a short time, wiped her nose again, and said, "Rick divorced me two years ago. He and Mama moved home, and she died a couple weeks ago. I was going to the funeral. No one wants me there, but I have to satisfy myself that I was the reason for so much strife and animosity and want so much to...have my own closure. And now I won't get that chance, right? Not much else to say. That's me in a nutshell."

No one said anything. Frank put his arm around

her shoulder trying to comfort her, but he knew it was just a kind gesture and nothing could change her feelings at this time.

She had to get this off her chest to someone, anyone, because those in Argentina will never know how she feels now.

After a while, Helen sat upright and said, "Okay, who's next?"

Soo Mi asked, "If you mind... Why didn't you have child?"

"I don't know. Sex was a physical thing. I don't think there was any love in it. I don't know what Rick felt. He never said much. I don't even know why I married him. Seemed to be the thing to do at the time, I guess."

There was silence on the raft—not the type that they had become used to, the one in which they would fall asleep. It was a silence of wonderment that someone took this specific time to bear her life story to complete strangers in such a life-threatening situation. Each passenger clearly mulled her story over and over in their minds, maybe trying desperately to understand their own lives within her story. Had they made the same mistakes? Had they judged someone as cruelly as Helen had to the point her life was now consumed by it? Would they be doing what she set out to do? Those questions were haunting Frank, and if he could answer one, another popped up unanswered. It was mind boggling.

Chapter Twenty

The unsettling silence eventually led to sleep, the crew once again being rocked into slumber by the action of the waves. Through the night, a gentle rain shower had filled their bottles through the makeshift funnels they had fashioned, and the flying fish were still in abundance for food.

As the sun rose, the crew began to awaken, each one going through the morning routine trying valiantly to avoid annoying the others with their quirks. Kimberly seemed especially isolated in her routine, her eyes darting back and forth from her tasks to the others around her as though she was waiting for one of them to enter her space. The others were totally ignorant of her actions, and this just seemed to push her more to perform quick, flicking motions as she repetitively tidied her space. It was virtually becoming not just repetitious but obsessive, maybe paranoid. Frank decided not to arouse anyone's attention to it.

Yuto was helping Soo Mi more than he had

before. She usually did most of the daily chores while Yuto helped Frank and Irving either plan for future problems or in dishing out portions of water and food. For some reason, Soo Mi was allowing him to clean 'house' more than usual, but the expressions on Yuto's face were not the normally bright look but more sad. Taking time to watch him closer, Frank noted tears flowing from his eyes, and Soo Mi, possibly hoping no one was watching, occasionally wiped them from his cheeks.

When Yuto and Soo Mi, almost simultaneously, noticed Frank and Helen looking at them in concern, Yuto cleared his throat and said to Helen, "You telling life to us last night on my mind all night. I, too, need to get things, how you say, 'off my body.'"

"That's 'off my chest,' Yuto," Irving intervened.

"Yes, so sorry for my English. My marriage to Soo Mi great dishonor on our families. We fall in love too fast and married too quick. Both of us have been shamed from living with family and now no money. How you say?"

"Disinherited?" Helen asked.

"Yes, Japanese man not marry Asian woman. Now we poor and work hard to make live, and now this crash has broken both our hearts and maybe our will," Yuto said, wiping tears from Soo Mi's eyes. "We not care for family wishes when we marry. We not like what they think."

"We not want sorry, but Helen show us telling your story may help us work with awful pain we have," Soo Mi finally said as she broke down in more tears.

~~ ~~ ~~

Being the closest to Soo Mi, Irving put his arms over Yuto's arm and around Soo Mi and tried his best to comfort these two who were obviously distraught over their family problems and now in this dire situation. Irving knew too well that family loyalty was often a necessary thing to have, but, at times, crossing the line in that loyalty often set many members apart and, for some, apart forever. All the feelings of being ostracized from any family affairs or events came flooding back to his psyche, causing him to hug the couple next to him even more, and for a period of time, longer than one would have expected.

Seeming somewhat embarrassed over their confessional, Yuto and Soo Mi sank into themselves for the rest of the day with only a few warm gazes toward Irving in thanks for his actions. Irving nodded back, accepting their gratitude.

Everyone else was back to their own thoughts as the sun rose above then began to set once again. Every once in a while, one crew member turned and leaned on the side of the raft and looked out to sea in an obvious, desperate attempt to find something other than water.

~~ ~~ ~~

"There, there, there it is! I see it!" screamed Kimberly, pointing to the right of the morning sun. "It's a boat. It's a boat!" she yelled and crawled up and almost over the side of the raft to the point that Helen had to grab hold of her to stop her from falling out.

Everyone scanned the water once again for any sign of a vessel, but the only thing Frank could see was several waves condensing together, possibly creating an image of a boat. He waited before stating the real facts so others would be able to figure it out for themselves. Kimberly kept creeping up the side of the raft, and Helen, and now Frank, restrained her from going overboard. Finally, the others conceded that Kimberly was once again making something up, and they turned to the center of the raft as Frank and Helen held Kimberly tight.

This is becoming a spectacle that's only going to get worse. Kimberly's hitting the wall!

Chapter Twenty-One

As the sunset stole the light from the ocean again, the crew, as always, snuggled closer to one another. It was an innate action—for fear of the night, warmth from the often chilly wind, or to be close to another human being in urgent times. The crew usually fell asleep at the same time. Only Frank fought it, trying to be the last to drift off, almost as a sentry goose that watches over its gaggle.

Soon all but Frank were asleep, all totally unaware of a floating object with dim running lights far out in the waters. The gusty wind was a bit more active this night, so the low hum of the vessel was not easily heard. The lighted object seemed to bob and heave with the waves as if going very slowly but deliberately.

Frank fully opened his sleepy eyes in a squint upon hearing what he thought were voices, but having slid down a bit behind the side of the raft, he was unable to see anything in the darkness. Again, there again, he heard what he thought were some voices but wrote it off to the sounds of the ocean and the raft playing tricks on him. Then the voices disappeared. He knew he was right to think he'd imagined it, and he dozed off into a light sleep.

Moments later, he awoke again, straining to hear and see, but there still was nothing. Then he heard the voices again, this time seemingly closer. The words were distinct but not English. The words were in Spanish. Frank thought this to be odd since, if he were dreaming, English would be the language spoken, even though he spoke fluent Spanish.

"Mira lo que tenemos aquí, mis amigos!" A husky voice.

A dim light shone over the raft.

Frank wanted to spring up and cheer, but he knew better.

Oh, my God, we are saved, but this isn't a very welcoming voice.

He didn't move. He also didn't want to let the person the voice belonged to know that he'd understood what had been said.

"Dejamos un grupo y, como magia, tenemos

otro. Esto debe ser Navidad, Héctor. ¡Nuestros patrocinadores adorarán estos regalos!" Frank heard and quickly translated it to: We drop off one group, and, like magic, we have another. This must be Christmas, Hector. Our sponsors will just love these presents!

What group? What presents? What sponsors. Who's Hector?

"Crees que están muertos? *(You think they're dead)*?" asked the second man. Hector?

"No. Creo que todavía están respirando. *(No. I think they are still breathing)*," said the first man.

Their boat gently nuzzled the raft, and Frank squinted his eyes open a bit, hoping to see what was going on without the visitors noticing he was awake.

They think we are alive!

The voice's figure stood with his legs apart on the bow of the boat, staring down into the raft and motioning for the second man to come forward. He had his upright index finger to his lips as if shushing him to be quiet. What was more intimidating than these actions were the shadows of gun barrels over their right shoulders. Two other human shadows appeared behind the men, but Frank could not hear what the first man said as he turned to them to give orders.

Suddenly, the boat's motor revved up and rammed the raft in an effort to rouse the crew. That was all they needed, and the survivors woke from their dreams to encounter their saviors. At first, Kimberly, Helen, and Soo Mi were gleeful, almost giddy, raising their arms in celebration. Yuto soon chimed in, but Frank saw Irving eyeing the men and their firearms and realized he knew better.

Irving wiggled over to Frank, and Frank whispered, "I speak Spanish but don't want them to know."

Irving immediately understood what the others didn't. They may be in more trouble than they had been floating at sea for the last several weeks.

"Buenas noche damas y caballeros. Que bueno verte. ¿por qué estás aquí? ¿Qué te ha pasado?"

Frank wanted to desperately answer, but he knew better. The man had asked, "Good evening, ladies and gentlemen. Good to see you. What are you doing here? What happened to you?" He hoped having them think none of them could understand Spanish would be an advantage to him to find out what they had in store for them.

As their eyes became accustomed to the light, the others seemed to notice that their knights in shining armor were not so lustrous and certainly not knights. The barrels of the weapons they were carrying were parts of AK-47s. The man who was talking was tall, bearded, and dressed in camouflage cargo pants, wearing a green rain slicker and a wide-brimmed hat with an accompanying lanyard around his neck. Those behind him were dressed in similar apparel and were also armed. Their bearded faces did not obscure their offensive demeanors. None of them were smiling. They looked over the passengers in the raft that had been minimized by the enormity of their vessel, and the more they scanned the inhabitants, the more they resembled a pack of jackals forming a plan of attack.

Irving took his cue from Frank and spoke, "No kaprannie Espanol."

Maybe he knew from his past experiences with the Shayetet 13, the elite fighting force of the Israeli

Army, that if there were more of these monsters, it would be some feat to conquer them all, especially with the weakened state of the crew members. The women would be of no help, and Yuto would particularly be homed in on protecting Soo Mi rather than effectively helping all to defeat this heavily armed bunch of pirates or, worse, murderers.

It looked, from the expression on Irving's face, that he had something to tell Frank. Did he want to divulge his past and plans to Frank? Irving inched over toward him, pretending to be repositioning himself to avoid the multiple lights being shone their way. The visitors were too engaged in tying up the raft and listening to the barking of orders by their leader's voice.

"I'm ex-Israeli special ops," Irving said. "I can help. You will need to follow my lead. Understand?"

"Yes," Frank, stunned by those words, said as he looked into Irving's eyes that spoke of his power, confidence, and hope.

"Amigos, my Ingles not so gud! You peoples get aqui. You hungry, no? We have comida, uh, food!"

the leader said slowly and deliberately. It was not a voice of caring but more of a warning of things to come.

Frank knew something was not right, but it was doubtful the others understood their situation yet. Once on their 'rescuer's' boat, they were likely to be prisoners, but they had no other choice. They were running out of fish and water, they had no nourishment to give them the strength to fight, much less think and move in a quick, coordinated manner, and they were exhausted. It was obvious they would have to endure the pirates' wishes and plans, at least until they could become stronger physically and mentally.

~~ ~~ ~~

Irving was the first to get to his feet, wobbling as the waves beat the raft against the other boat's hull. He extended his hand out to one of the helpers, clasped his forearm as the man's hand grasped his arm, placed his right foot on the side of the raft, and, using the raft as a trampoline, attempted to bounce up as the pirate tried to hoist him aboard.

This technique allowed Irving to evaluate the strength of this man. As he came on board, Irving looked his adversary's face over to place his features into a mental database for the future, a technique that was considered a 'must' in his training. He then pretended to fall toward another crew member in order to test that man's strength as well.

At this point, Irving turned to help his friends, but he was pushed away aggressively by the leader.

"Retroceder (*back*)! Move! Alli (*there*)!"

Irving did not resist. He knew better.

One by one, each passenger was brought on board the rescue boat and were gradually aligned in a line on the bow facing the center console and the commander. Soo Mi clung to Yuto, Kimberly and Helen held hands, and Frank stood next to Irving, all waiting for the next order to be given. The other pirates stared at the man in the cargo pants and green slicker who had just exposed his entire AK-47 in front of him.

"You need eat, now!" He waved his hands to his men who started to herd the survivors past the console and the steps to below.

~~ ~~ ~~

The passengers tried to keep upright, but the boat, with its engines idling in the water, pitched in multiple directions, and they lurched against the side wall of the stairs as they finally reached the bottom floor of the vessel. An old wooden table with benches around it and a small kitchen in the back welcomed them, and one of the men was hustling around behind a counter, moving dishes and opening cabinets and putting portions of food from containers onto plates. Another man motioned to them to sit and then went to get plastic glasses and put them in front of each person. A pink fluid was poured into the glasses, and the plates were served with fish, crackers, and rice with a thick gravy on top. Despite the overall distasteful appearance of the food, the survivors ate every morsel. They drank the fluid and even held their glasses up, asking for more, never really knowing what the drink was.

All the time, Frank was thinking where they were to sleep and how they were going to fare on this boat. Would they be tied up? Would they be made to work? Where would they be going? As he finished his drink, he peered over his glass at Irving and felt he had the same concerns, as he, too, stared back for a fleeting second before the boss spoke.

"Todo terminado (*Everything finished*)? Estómagos llenos (*full stomachs*)?" He rubbed his stomach and belted out a laugh, more sinister than fun-loving. "OK, amigos, up! Now go siesta, yes?"

Again, his helpers rounded everyone up, aiming them down a hallway to one big room with three bunks on one side and three on the other. Helen and Kimberly took the right side immediately, but Soo Mi hung back, trying to cling to Yuto, but was pulled away by Hector, gently but forcibly pushing her to the right and simultaneously shoving Yuto to the left where the other men stood.

"Debes dormir ahora (*You must sleep now*)," the leader said with a raspy gargle. "You, cama, uh, bed, now!" He pointed to the bunks on both sides of the cabin.

Irving quickly followed the orders, got in the upper bunk, and everyone else, including Frank, followed. Hector stood watch, and it wasn't long before the rest of them were all asleep. Did any of the others hear the cabin door shut and lock behind them?

Chapter Twenty-Two

As Irving began to doze off, the terror of this new situation brought back memories filled with images of a previous time. There they crouched, his entire commando group. They huddled together to organize as they appeared from nowhere out of the sea. The assassination of an Hezbollah cleric was the only thing on their minds. They had trained for it and were intensely ready for the mission. They had landed in the dark and were now progressing inland to their prescribed destination. Every man had his duty memorized and had practiced for this very moment for months. Irving was concentrating on his part of it. He was the lead man of the second group assigned to take out any enemy that should threaten the first commando group who were setting up and separating to perform an entry tunnel for the rest.

Then all hell had broken loose. The entire group had been detected, and an ambush of Hezbollah and Amal fighters was everywhere, firing their AK-47s unmercifully into their ranks with no relief in sight. Booby traps exploded all around him. His leader was killed instantly. Others died from the detonations of their own explosives they were carrying. Chaos continued, bullets whizzing to and fro as the remaining soldiers took as much cover as possible.

Irving had almost been out of ammo. He sought the ammunition of others who were lying dead around him. He felt like panicking, running, dodging bullets and explosives, but he knew better.

"Keep calm, man."

In the distance, Irving thought he heard the roar of helicopters, but mortars continued to erupt, full auto ammunition rang out, and screaming and unintelligible language continued throughout the night.

Irving huddled down in a flat secluded spot, lying on his back awaiting death, and then the sound of a friendly voice woke him, and he bolted straight up.

"What?" he whispered. "How many are dead?" he asked.

"No one, Irving, it's me, Frank. No one has come back, and everyone is asleep. You were dreaming, man. Jesus, back with the Israelis, uh?"

"Yeah, yeah. Eleven of sixteen dead. God, I gotta get my shit together," Irving whispered.

"They have not tied us up. I guess they're thinking we are not very strong to take them outright, especially with the three women," Frank said.

"Yeah, we'll need to use that to our advantage somehow. Hopefully, at least one or two of the others will cooperate and distract them. We need more time to evaluate this boat. I don't even know what size it is, what kind of motors, how many, who's running it. Gotta think," Irving said.

"I can help. Just tell me what to do or what to look for," Frank said, patting Irving on the shoulder as he rolled back in his bunk and faced the hull.

Irving shook his head to rid himself of the Ansariya mission's misery in Lebanon. It had become a recurring nightmare and rightfully so. He and four others out of sixteen combat brothers were able to get out alive that night in 1997. He took a deep breath, rubbed his eyes, turned over, and tried to sleep again.

Chapter Twenty-Three

"Buenos dias, amigos (*Good morning, friends*)!" the commander barked. He was standing in the doorway of their cabin, and all Frank could see was a ghostly shadow of a figure, his features being blocked out by the sun behind him. "Es la hora del desayuno (*It is breakfast time*)!" he barked again, motioning with his hands repetitively from his stomach to his mouth.

This motion was universal, and slowly everyone got out of their bunks while glancing at each other. They were all bound to be so very hungry, and Frank reckoned their captors knew it as well. Frank tried to tell the others near him not to be fooled by this man and his pirates but was cut short by the bellowing of the leader.

"Hey! No hables ahora (*Do not speak now*)!" His angry face was evident as he put his right index finger up to his pursed lips. "Shhhh!"

With that order, the passengers aligned themselves, innately allowing the women to leave their cabin. They were then hustled to the room where they had eaten the night before and pushed through the door one by one. The long table had already been set with utensils and napkins, and each of them were motioned to sit. A rank cup of black coffee, some type of gruel, and a flat piece of bread were placed in front of them.

As they ate, Hector spoke sharply, "Atención!" while holding his left arm out, wrist bent up, and his palm facing them. They all immediately stopped eating. He then crossed his chest with a benediction sign and motioned them to continue.

His actions were not considered important as they resumed eating, but Irving was looking at Hector intently. Had he noticed a few things about him? He made a quick glance at Frank, who was always awaiting any signal from Irving, who then raised his left hand up and down at the wrist. Obviously, Hector was one man who would have to be dealt with if they were to obtain their freedom. Frank nodded as he continued to eat. Unfortunately, the food was not appetizing, but it was sustenance for all of the passengers.

The other two pirates remained in the room as they ate. Everyone took their time doing so, as if they'd finally realized something about their rescue was not right. Everyone but Kimberly. She scoffed down her food and the bad coffee and then held her plate out for more. Not one of their captors made a move to do anything.

Kimberly insisted by continuously pushing out her plate and saying, "Please, please!"

The nearest pirate finally shoved the plate back at her, but she wasn't going to have any of his actions.

She stood and said, "I'm still famished. Please, please, more food!"

Frank spoke softly, "Kimberly, sit down. They are not going to feed us a lot. Please, sit down."

"I don't understand. They saved us. They will take care of us, and when we get to land, we will be returned home." Kimberly spoke with a fervent belief that these men were her saviors.

Frank felt that this was not the time or the situation to try to calm her down, so he leaned back from the table and said nothing. Kimberly continued speaking but was ignored by the guards until she became belligerent by standing up and still pushing her plate toward them. One of them finally had his fill of her antics and slapped the plate from her hand. The tin plate slammed to the floor once it bounced off the bench, and a stillness suddenly came over the entire room. It was clear at this time that all of them realized these men were not their liberators, but who were they?

The boss was now standing in the doorway, having been summoned by one of the guards. "No more food! Levántate (*Get up*). Ven conmigo (*Come with me*)," he said as he motioned everyone.

They again glanced at Frank and Irving as if waiting for other instructions. Irving waved at them to follow. Irving gestured to Frank to get in the front of the line. Frank knew Irving wanted to check out the rest of the boat as he had mentioned it to him earlier, so Frank positioned himself as the second person in line and purposely walked slowly to give Irving time to get a good look at their surroundings.

Frank timed the boat's sudden lurch against a wave to stumble and fall to one knee to give Irving more time to purvey the boat's configuration. There were multiple compartments other than the mess hall. Their accommodations were in the hull below. As they passed down the corridor, Frank noted 'Sala de máquinas' on the door. *The engine room.* He stumbled again, this time putting his left hand against the engine room's sign, hoping Irving would understand there was a significance to his actions.

His actions were not wasted. Irving picked up on his signal, but he also was able to pick out the communication room where there were radios and other communication equipment. Frank hoped Irving was making a mental note of these, too. Would he also feign being wobbled by the boat's rocking motion in order to seek more information about the craft?

Finally, they were herded up another staircase to the deck, initially blinded by the sun as it shone from the cloudless sky. As his eyes accommodated to the light, all Frank could see was sea and sky, no land. Their raft had been tied to the back of the pirates' boat. Suddenly the engines came to life as the vessel jerked forward, knocking several of the passengers off balance, causing them to crouch onto the deck, grabbing for anything to keep them steady. Their captors laughed at the sight of these gringos flopping on the deck like clowns, trying to keep their balance.

They were on their way, but where?

Chapter Twenty-Four

Soo Mi looked around at the others as they slept in their assigned bunks. She concentrated on everyone, one by one, to be sure they were truly asleep. Slowly pushing away the gray-blue blanket covering her, she slid her legs on the side of the bunk and slipped silently to the floor. She felt Kimberly turn to the hull's side as she stood next to her bunk. She hesitated to be sure Kimberly was not waking. Satisfied, she peeked through the slit of the makeshift curtain her captives had made between the men and women and eyed Yuto's bunk. Luckily, he was on the bottom, and this made it easy for her to get to it and nestle in next to him. He woke and, seeing her face, moved closer to the wall to allow her space. He held her tight, smelling her hair and caressing her face.

"Are you okay?" he asked softly.

She shook her head up and down while raising her index finger to her pursed lips.

He placed his lips to her ear and whispered, "No

place to go. We will have to wait. I love you and will protect you."

She looked longingly into his eyes and nodded once again. "I never leave your side. We are as one." And then she lifted her lips to his and kissed him.

They both hugged each other tightly until they loosened their grips and fell asleep.

Soo Mi woke with a start as the boat lurched over the waves. No one else seemed to react. She had no idea how long she had been with Yuto. She slowly stood, covered him with his blanket, and made her way through the curtain to the women's side. As she prepared to stand on the side of Kimberly's bunk, Kimberley softly grabbed her foot and rose up, looked around as if she didn't know where she was, and whispered, "Are you trying to get us all killed? They will kill us, you know. I am going to get off this boat as soon as I can. I know you are scheming with them."

"No, I was—" Soo Mi was cut short by Kimberly's response.

"Yes, you were, but I'm not going to tell the others because I know they are doing it, too. I don't think you will kill me. Let me die the way I want to."

"Please, go back to sleep. I not interested ever hurting you. You must believe that."

Before Soo Mi could prepare to respond to Kimberly's next reply, she noticed Kimberly's eyes were closed and she was breathing with slow, deep breaths. She realized Kimberly's response was not a conscious one, but it certainly heralded a deep-seated paranoia within Kimberly, and this frightened Soo Mi.

Soo Mi ascended to her bunk, pulled the blanket over her, and stared at the ceiling of their compartment while the others slept.

~~ ~~ ~~

She did not realize that Irving had watched her closely.

~~ ~~ ~~

All the passengers were awakened the next morning with an unusual sound that was nothing like the boat motors that had hummed throughout the night. They all strained to identify the sound as they held themselves up in their bunks on their elbows.

"What is that?" Helen asked.

"It's an airplane, prop type, I think," said Irving.

"Where the hell are we?" asked Kimberly.

No one answered. No one knew. Slowly they all dressed and tried to align themselves toward the closed cabin doors that had been locked every night they had been aboard. Then they waited as the airplane seemed to circle the boat.

"Could that be a plane looking for us? What will they do if that plane *is* looking for us? Will the plane contact them? What will they do to us?" Helen droned on.

"It could be one of theirs, too," Frank said.

"Damn, I didn't think of that," Helen replied softly.

Suddenly, the cabin door flew open. "Buenos Dias, amigos!" said the leader from above. "Sube las escaleras, vamonos (*Go up the stairs, let's go*)!"

Almost everyone understood this command, and like soldiers, they marched up to the next level for food. Frank gave a fleeting glance to Irving, and he knew Irving also understood—that plane was not searching for them, for sure.

Chapter Twenty-Five

"Cuantos tienes (*How many do you have*)?" came the voice from the radio in the communications cabin.

"Seis (*six*)," answered the radio man.

"Mujeres (*women*)?"

"Tres (*three*)."

"Estan viejos (*They are old*)?" spoke the voice again.

"No."

"Bueno. Nos pondremos en contacto con usted. Adios (*Good. We will contact you. Goodbye*)," said the voice over the radio.

And then there was silence.

Frank heard this conversation as he passed the radio room to breakfast.

So they want to know if we were old. Thank God for that. They would have killed any old ones. The number of women? Yep, they're up to no good.

As he was pondering the conversation, he realized the airplane noise was no longer present.

That's their communication to their sponsors. Our destiny awaits us for sure as soon as that plane returns.

At breakfast, Frank tried to get Irving's attention to tell him of the news. It was difficult because the pirates had mixed the women with the men, separating Frank from Irving. Irving was always looking for something from Frank, and he tapped his fingers on the table while reaching for his drink. Frank realized this as an attempt to find out anything new. Frank knocked after waiting for a period of time to pass. One tap for news, two taps for none. He tapped once. Irving nodded and wiped his mouth with a napkin, then repeated the action several times. Frank figured that Irving wanted him to take napkins with him, but why? Then Irving put the napkin down and pulled his index finger across it back and forth. Frank got the message that they could speak to each other by writing on the napkins and passing them to one another since their captors always wanted silence from them.

But what will we write with?

He faced Irving after being sure he wasn't being

watched and raised his eyes as if questioning Irving's actions. Irving nodded. Frank positioned his fingers as if writing with his thumb and index finger together, flat on the table. Irving clearly understood his concern by giving a 'thumbs up' sign. It wasn't the usual thumb sign but a pinky slightly elevated as he drank from his cup.

Frank thought Irving had a way of getting something to write with so he knew he just had to wait. But when and how could Irving get a pencil without those goons seeing him? They were always around watching, and it was unnerving for Frank that one slip-up would mean they would be tied up and shut up in their cabin for the rest of the trip.

There weren't that many napkins on the table and they were not neatly placed for each passenger. Helen was by his right side, so he touched her leg to get her attention. She looked up, and he motioned to her to get a napkin by reaching for one for himself. As she did so, he tapped her leg twice to stop her immediate reaction.

Take your time. We don't want to let them get suspicious.

He was amazed that she stopped her grab for the napkins and instead reached for a glass of orange juice and waited for a good period of time before obtaining two napkins that just happened to be stuck together. There was a twinkle in her eye as she tilted her head to eye him. He knew she was on the same page as he. From now on, Helen was ready to help.

That's three of us!

~~ ~~ ~~

The weather was bright, sunny, and warm. The water from the bow splashing back over them was warm as well. Their captors had allowed them a small window of time to get up on deck and get some relief from being kept isolated below. As Frank and the others looked around from the sides and back of the craft, all Frank could see was ocean. The boat was seemingly at top speed and certainly was not slowing. They were on an obvious time schedule to get to wherever they were going.

Irving positioned himself next to Frank by pretending to look over the side of the boat, acting like a tourist on a tour. "Anything?" he said to Frank.

"Human traffickers," Frank replied.

Irving let his head slump farther, signaling his disappointment. He then stood and walked behind Frank. Frank responded in kind and moved toward the area previously occupied by Irving.

"Must be going to land," Irving whispered. "Will need a plan after we get there." Irving pointed to a swell in the water as if he was showing Frank something in the ocean to cover their conversation as small talk.

"Napkins?" Frank asked as he, too, pointed to the same swell.

"Yep!" Irving sidled slowly away after the boat hit a high wave, and he stumbled to catch his balance.

Frank still had no idea how he was going to write on his napkin. As he turned around to scan the top deck of the boat, he noticed that Irving wasn't there anymore. He had disappeared. The guards were still standing around the passengers and seemed unaware he was gone.

What the hell?

As he searched for him, Frank became uneasy. Irving was a cog in the wheel of success that they could not afford to lose. Where was the commander and Hector? Had they grabbed him? No one was showing any signs of uneasiness. The guards were the same, stone-cold faced without showing any anxiety or change in emotion. Suddenly, there was Irving, looking up at the sun with his eyes closed as if sunning his face and attempting to get a tan. His index finger was touching his thumb as he placed them in a circular motion on the railing of the boat.

Frank then closed his eyes and tried to get a tan as well.

Chapter Twenty-Six

The weather had changed so quickly. It was as if they had entered a tunnel. The clouds were dark, the wind blew in uneven circular patterns, and the boat was tossed to and fro. The passengers were hustled down to their bunk room, told to keep quiet and get into their bunks. A guard stood at the door, although he was having a great deal of difficulty keeping his balance. After a while, it became apparent the he had had it with this job, and he closed the door and left.

All Frank heard was a key enter the lock of the door and the turning of the tumblers. There was silence among them, and slowly Irving got up. While holding on to the bunks and the hull, he eased over to the door and placed his ear on it. He stood there for a while, changing his ear position several times. Then he turned and faced the rest and shook his head from side to side, signifying there was no one outside the door. He placed his index finger to his lips and softly whispered, "Shhh!"

Frank responded to Irving's hand motion to come closer to him.

So we're to be auctioned off or what? Irving wrote on a napkin with a small pencil he had stolen the day before, then handed the napkin to Frank with the pencil.

Traffickers, no idea what they are going to do or when they're going to do it. Plane to give orders now they know we're valuable candidates to sell Frank wrote then passed the napkin back to Irving.

Irving read the note, crushed it in his hand, and whispered, "Well, that means we have to start organizing quickly. We have no idea how many of these goons there are on land. There are four of them on this boat. I expect there are at least four AKs here as well. I know I can take out two of them, but it will be hard because of the number of us and three women who will not be able to physically engage with them. I don't know much about Yuto. Would be great if he knew karate, but I'm not betting on it."

"I can ask, but I'm thinking like you. The women are the biggest problem, and Kimberly has been acting loco as of late, and I'm afraid she could be losing it. Just look at her over there all hunched up on her bunk. She really hasn't been communicating with the others, even when we're alone. I think she really thought these guys were saving us."

"Yeah, I've noticed," Irving responded.

Frank eased his way over to Yuto and Soo Mi. *Any experience in fighting?* he wrote on another napkin.

"I hold my own," Yuto replied softly. "Just because I Japanese not mean I know karate, if dat what you mean, but I think I hold own when needed."

Soo Mi whispered, "Only Kung Fu. Me beginner. Only for exercise. I know not how fight."

"I understand. Thanks. Good to know," Frank acknowledged. "Everyone, come here," he beckoned.

Everyone slowly got out of their bunks and surrounded Frank. Kimberly did not, so Frank walked over to her bunk and tapped her on the shoulder as she faced the hull. She did not respond right away. He tapped again.

"Please, Kimberly, this is important. Come on over." He returned to the group, and Kimberly grudgingly slipped down from her bunk and joined them as Irving once again listened at the door.

"We are really in trouble here. I think these guys are human traffickers," Frank said.

Some of the group gasped quietly.

"That plane we heard a while back? I think that's their contact, and they will be back now that they know we're on board," Frank said.

"How do you know this?" asked Kimberly, surprising everyone.

"I speak Spanish, but they don't know it. I was able to hear their communications to the plane."

"Oh, God, I'm going to be raped and beaten and sold?" Kimberly blurted as she jumped back away from the group.

Helen hurried and held her to her side. "Not if we can help one another."

"We have to be calm and resolute here," Frank said forcefully. "All of our lives will depend on what we say and do in the future. Do not let them know we know anything. Don't tell them I understand Spanish. Act accordingly. Follow their orders and don't give them anything to get them mad at us. If one of us goes nuts, no telling what they will do to all of us."

Irving once again listened at the door intently then turned to the others. "We will need to overpower these guys somehow. We will need to pick the place and time, but time may not be on our side. They are taking us to land as far as I can tell. This could be good or bad. Bad because there may be more of them to get away from, or good in that we will have more options to choose from if there are only four of them there. We need to keep attention on that plane when it returns, and Frank needs to hear the transmission from the plane to translate their intentions. Everyone here needs to be on their toes, so if anyone hears the plane, somehow you must let Frank know."

"How?" Yuto asked.

"We need a sign to let him know if he doesn't hear it first. If you hear the plane, find Frank as soon as possible and place your hands behind your head as if massaging your neck and slide your hands over your ears like this. Got it?" Irving said, looking at each person, and it was obvious he was specifically awaiting any negative response as he repeated the signal motion three times.

"What if we not together when plane come?" Soo Mi asked.

"Use the sign to others, and, hopefully, we can get the message to Frank. He then has to get near the radio room to hear at the same time, so it won't be easy, but it is the only way we can know their plans," Irving answered.

A key was turning in the lock. They all scurried to their bunks, each pretending to be curled up and sleeping. Frank pocketed the napkin and settled on his back with his hands clasped behind his head as the guard entered the room.

"Levántate!"

Frank knew the others did not know he wanted them all up, so he raised his head and motioned to the guard and said, "No Espanol."

The guard responded by raising his hand up and down, the up signal being more prominent.

"Levántate!"

Shrugging as if guessing what he meant, Frank got up and told the others to get out of their bunks. They were herded out the door one by one and down the corridor past the radio room and the other living quarters. Irving appeared to be counting the number of steps to the radio room. Just in case he needed to get there in the dark?

The passengers had been so engaged in their scheming that they didn't notice the weather had subdued, and the boat was now again at full speed to a destination. They were ushered into another cabin where the boss was sitting behind a fancy desk with his feet up on its right side, smoking a cigar and smiling.

"Buenas tardes, amigos (*Good afternoon, friends*)! You like dis boat ride mucho?"

No one answered, and suddenly he sat up, dropped his feet to the floor, and yelled, "Buenas Tardes, amigos! You like dis boat ride mucho?"

Surprisingly, Yuto responded before Frank could think. "Where we go?"

"Ah! Alguien ahora habla (*Someone now*

speaks)! You no American, eh? De Japon, eh? Where we go?" The leader laughed in a sinister manner. "How you say? Me know, you not know? Pero sabrás pronto (*But you will know soon*)," he said between heavy laughter.

So this bastard isn't going to tell us. Either he knows or he's waiting for his orders.

"You son of a bitch!" Kimberly screamed. "Who the hell do you think you are? Where the hell are we going? You have no right to abduct us, you bastard." She quickly approached the man whose laughter suddenly halted as he stood and smacked her in the face. Kimberly lost her balance and fell against the edge of the desk.

"Cállate mujer (*Shut up, woman*)! Estoy a cargo aquí (*I'm in charge here*). Eres mi prisionero (*You are my prisoner*)!"

Helen rushed over to help Kimberly to her feet as the boss pushed both of them back into line.

Christ! No doubt about it now. He's a prick, not going to take any guff from anyone, and we are indeed now officially his prisoners.

Helen gathered up some rags off a shelf nearby

to apply some pressure to the small bleeding cut on Kimberly's head. One of the guards, obviously emboldened by their boss' actions, ripped one of them from her hand, but she was able to hold on to the other, burying Kimberly's head under her arm so the guard couldn't get to it.

"Ahora que sabes quién está a cargo, me escucharás a mí y a mis hombres (*Now that you know who is in charge, you will listen to me and my men*). Harás exactamente lo que te digan y nada más (*You will do exactly what they tell you and nothing else*). Lo entiendes (*You understand*)?"

"Please," said Irving. "No speak Espanol!"

"Me boss. You do what I say! Entiéndeme? You know?"

"Yes, we understand," said Irving as he held out his arms in a submissive posture, indicating that all of them understood. He then said to the rest, "He's the boss. No arguing." And then he turned to the commander and nodded in the affirmative.

"Bien, todos somos amigos ahora (*Well, we are all friends now*)?" the boss said.

Yeah, sure, we are all your friends, asshole, but

only until we can get the hell out of here somehow.

They were once again roughly ushered back to the sleeping quarters with Helen still attending to Kimberly's head. Soo Mi and Yuto were first allowed to use the toilet within their cabin, but as soon as they were finished, the guard checked all of them visually, slammed the door, and locked it.

"Kimberly. You okay?" Frank asked.

"Those bastards. What else do we have to endure? The fucking crash, eating each other, starving half to death, sharks, and now these idiots. I want to kill them. I hate them. You understand?"

"We all feel this way, Kimberly, but if we all act like you, they will have no qualms about eliminating us all. Get yourself together. Calm yourself down, please," said Irving, hugging her as Helen let her loose.

"I'll get those bastards, if it's the last thing I do," Kimberly said.

"Kimberly, please!" Helen said softly.

Chapter Twenty-Seven

Banging on the locked door woke the survivors. It was time for breakfast. The usual coffee with thick grinds at the bottom of the cup, powdered eggs, and orange juice were served every morning. Frank guessed that it was around seven or eight o'clock. The guards had taken anything worth money when they'd been rescued, including Irving's watch. Frank had slipped his into a secret pocket in his cargo pants before they'd confiscated their valuables. He never looked at it unless he was alone.

As they lined up to go out the door, the guard halted them from exiting and pointed to Frank and Yuto to come with him. Again, they walked down the corridor past the radio room. Frank tried to estimate the area of their cabin where he could choose as the best place to hear the communications if he were in their cabin by counting the steps again from their door.

They entered the boss' cabin and were placed in front of the desk. The guard left them there alone.

They both looked at each other, Frank questioning himself.

The boss finally entered with great fanfare. "Buenos dias, amigos!"

Having witnessed his displeasure before when no one answered, Frank faked a terrible Spanish accent and repeated, "Bunos dyas!"

The boss laughed, amused instead of angered by the response.

"You never see America again, you know?"

"What?" Yuto asked.

"No see America! We sell you!"

Frank didn't want to converse in Spanish as severely as he wanted for fear of exposing his ability to understand their plans. He almost blurted out a long answer in Spanish but held back.

"America has more money for you," Frank finally explained. "We have amigos with dinero, much dinero!"

The boss laughed and snickered. "No good America dinero. Escupo sobre eso (*I spit on that*)," he said in a nasty manner as he spit on the floor.

"What now?" Yuto asked.

"You know today. Tell la mujer shut up or..." The boss put his index finger to his temple and pulled it back like a trigger.

"Please—" Frank said but was cut off.

"No. No. You no talk! Tell all shut up!" the boss demanded.

After getting back to their quarters, Frank let everyone know that they were truly in trouble and that their plans would have to be made up quickly. He did not voice his deep concerns about Kimberly because he knew if she spoke up one more time, it would be a disaster for her and all of them, really.

He sat on the lower bunk with Irving and asked, "Well, what's your plan?"

"We've been hauling ass for a long time and not near shore. I'm wondering if there is a rendezvous with another ship. I still think we need to wait for the plane's instructions," Irving said.

"Jesus, this is nerve-racking for us. I can't imagine what is for the others," Helen remarked.

A noise at the door distracted them from their conversation. Another guard opened the door and motioned them all out of the cabin. They entered the breakfast area, all looking at one another, wondering why they were here in the middle of the afternoon.

The commander entered, this time with a jovial demeanor. "Es hora de celebrar a nuestros amigos (*It's time to celebrate, our friends*). ¡Saca la cerveza (*Take out the beer*)!"

Celebrate what? Beer?

The other guards brought bottles of beer in cases, opened them, and gave one to each person. Everyone imbibed while questioning the motive of the boss. He, too, was drinking and flirting with Kimberly and Helen, both of whom were obviously standoffish with him, but he didn't seem to care. Hector tried to flirt with Soo Mi, but Yuto stepped between them and offered a sip of his beer. The guard backed off after seeing the boss motioning him away.

Irving moved closer to the boss and asked, "Why we celebrate?"

"Ah ha, we soon know pedidos and dis will be over!"

Soo Mi suddenly bumped into Irving, the

closest person to her, and put her hands behind her head and slid them over her ears. Irving stood still and listened. It was a little difficult to hear because of the noise from the celebrating crew, but Frank thought he heard it, too. Irving elbowed Frank, who was passing by, and gave the same signal. Frank lifted his head and, yes, he heard it again. As if on cue, he maneuvered toward Helen and said, "It's plane time. I'm gonna pretend to get sick and need to go to the corridor."

Frank then turned his back to the group, put his finger down his throat after taking three quick large swigs of beer, and immediately threw up and dropped to his knees. Helen reached for him and pretended to be very concerned for his health as the guards stood around laughing. She helped him out of the room and down the corridor, where Frank dropped to the floor outside the radio room and heaved up some more beer and faked passing out. Helen started to cry and consoled his now-still body. One of the guards, who followed, watched intently and, seeing Frank pass out, laughed, swigged some beer, and returned to the mess hall.

The sound of the propellers of the plane became quite obvious now as it was attempting to circle the boat, and the radio's speaker spouted a fast-speaking Spanish voice. "Procede a Playa de Redinha, luego al norte veintiocho kilómetros a lo largo de la costa. Llegue a la hora asignada fuera de la costa, a un kilómetro de la costa y confirme con la señal. Transferirá a los prisioneros a la orilla. ¿Entender?"

The radio operator responded, "Si!" and repeated the directions word for word.

All the while, the 'unconscious' Frank was listening and recording the words in his mind. *Proceed to Playa de Redinha, then north twenty-eight kilometers along the coast. Arrive at designated time off the coast, one kilometer from the coast and confirm with signal. Will transfer the prisoners to the shore. Understand?*

Shit, that means we're somewhere near the coastline of South America. Brazil. We're going to be transferred, and that ain't good!

He opened his eyes, caught a glimpse of Helen but no one else, and, making sure he was correct, he waited a few seconds before moving and said, "Ain't good. We're going to Brazil and being transferred to land."

"Oh, my God!" Helen whispered. "When?"

"Didn't get a time. Was probably already designated before the transmission."

Chapter Twenty-Eight

Once the 'celebration' was over, the boss commanded his goons to return the captors to their cabin. The door was closed and locked. Irving, as usual, placed his right ear on the door. He had done this so many times that the rest of the passengers probably didn't even give it a second thought. He never listened and heard anyone, so why now? As he changed his position, he stopped at one place on the door, pressed closer, and with his left hand kept violently waving it in silence until he had everyone's attention. Then, in the stillness, he turned and leaned quietly on the door.

He pointed to it and held up two fingers and then pretended to shoot the ceiling.

Two goons outside the door. They're listening to us.

Frank raised his index finger to his lips, pulled the napkin out of his pocket and shook it, and then motioned to Irving by placing his index finger and thumb together and putting them on the flat surface of a bunk rail. Irving reached into his pocket and retrieved the pencil. Frank folded the napkin and wrote exactly what he'd heard so everyone understood the severity of the situation. They weren't sure what time it was, but they were certain that this night their lives would change big time.

Irving listened to the door again and again, and finally signaled all clear after being doubly sure no one was outside the door. He approached Frank. "Here's the thing. Somehow they need to get us on something to transfer us. If it is a little boat, a Zodiac or smaller, then I would think we are being taken to land, but if they come out with a larger vessel, then that could mean we are being shipped somewhere."

"So what can we do?" Frank asked clearly and decisively.

"Once the door is opened by one of the goons, I'll pull him into the room, break his neck, and take his AK. If there are two of them, we might have a problem. So far, we have only had one goon come, but this is the transfer, so we may have two. I will need you and Yuto to help with the first one I drag into the room if there are two. You will need to cut his throat." Irving stared straight at Frank and then Yuto.

"What? With what? How?" Yuto gasped quietly.

Irving pulled his pants leg up and retrieved the scalpel he had used on the raft from his sock.

"This! It has to be a deep cut right away so there isn't any noise from his throat to warn anyone else. The throat needs to be cut clean through. I really mean clean through, got it? If only one guy, I can take care of that, and then we will take each guy one at a time. I'm sure the boss will be driving the boat and his helper should be communicating with the pickup vessel. That gives us time to kill two of them, get two AKs, and deal with the other two. From there, we hijack the boat and get the hell out of here."

No sooner had Irving finished speaking, the door flew open, shocking everyone.

The boss man was standing in the doorway. "Get in bed, stay! Bad rain come. Nobody move!" The door slammed shut, the lock clicked, but not before Frank noted only one guard behind the leader.

"Bad weather good for us. It make their job a more hard, I think," said Yuto.

Irving smiled and nodded. Yuto was right. The irregular rocking boat made it more unsteady for the guards since they needed to tote their AK-47s with them wherever they went and also needed to carry heavy magazines as well.

Irving put one hand on Frank's shoulder and the other on Yuto's back and said, "If I pull the guard in it is because there are two of them. You must make sure the AK is vertical, not across his chest, otherwise the gun will block him from getting into the room. It won't fit through the door being horizontal. This is a small entrance," he said, pointing to the locked door.

They both nodded in the affirmative.

Helen and Soo Mi were intently listening to every word spoken. Kimberly was bent over in bed.

"What can we do?" Helen asked.

"Use this knife to cut up long pieces of those extra sheets over there so we can use them to tie them up if need be," Irving said. "Be sure to hide any extra pieces so they don't see any remnants of the sheets. Then give everyone as many as you can equally. Don't forget to get the knife back to me."

Helen and Soo Mi immediately started their task and soon had multiple strands of sheets distributed to the others and returned the knife to Irving. He neatly replaced it inside his sock after wrapping the blade to protect him from the sharp edge. The boat rocked back and forth, an indication for the worsening weather ahead.

Frank and Yuto went over the physical activities they may need to silence one of the guards. They had never killed anyone in their lives, they said. The idea of slashing a person's throat as deeply as Irving described was something out of some horror movie. Of course, in the movies, the blood spurting out of the neck was the center of the viewers' attention, not the throat being cut in half. What if they were unable to do it? Did one of them have to slash the throat again? How was one to know if the breathing tube was cut enough? They both had questions, some of them easy to answer and others so difficult to imagine. Their conversation came to an end as they were thrown out of their bunks against the hull next to the door. Each passenger crawled back into their bunks and held on for dear life.

Kimberly was now eyeing everyone as they moved to get into their bunks. It was as though she hadn't heard a word of their plans and didn't care.

Chapter Twenty-Nine

Overnight, the seas had become rougher and rougher, and the engines had slowed. Whoever was driving the boat had to take on the waves one by one and not worry about getting to their rendezvous point.

As the morning sun brightened their cabin, Frank noticed the boat was not lurching as much and, in fact, the engines had increased in speed. He looked through a small porthole on the hull and saw there were blue skies.

"The worst is over for now. Don't know where we are or how much farther it is, but I think we are going to initiate our escape soon," he said.

"Okay, let's line up and see how this plan will roll out. We just can't afford for anyone to be in the way of myself and Frank and Yuto," Irving said. "This has to go smoothly. The second guy will be mine. I will throw the first toward you, and then one of you must grab his head, jerk it back, and the other cuts his throat. The other must wait to see if the goon's hands go up to his neck or if he is trying to get to his gun. His hands to his head must be stopped. If he is more interested in his gun, grab the gun and hold it steady until his throat is cut. Got it? Remember, the AK needs to be vertical, up and down, right? Let's go through it slow motion."

Frank gestured how he would cut the throat, and Yuto nodded. Irving faced them and pretended to be off balance, stumbling toward them. Yuto could not get out of the way fast enough, and Irving stood upright.

"That's not going to work, Yuto. You must be totally out of the way. Stand up against this side of the door and wait until you can direct the gun up as he passes you," Irving said.

Yuto nodded again.

They went through their plan of the attack over and over until Irving felt they had the gist of it. "Now practice it more when you can. It has to go right," said Irving.

Then, a knock on the door, and Hector said, "Banos?"

It was time for the usual bathroom breaks.

Irving grabbed his knife, gave it to Frank, and positioned himself at the door. Yuto stood against the sidewall, Frank a few steps behind him.

"Okay," said Frank.

"Envía a las damas primero (*Send the ladies first*). Solo mujeres (*Only women*)! Wee-man."

Irving quickly looked at Frank and Yuto and whispered, "No go!"

Then he waved to Frank to hide the knife and pulled Helen and Soo Mi from their bunks and led them to the door. Just as the door opened fully, Kimberly bolted from her bunk, knocking aside Helen and Soo Mi, screaming expletives and ripping violently at the pirate's clothing and then his face. He backed up, off balance, and fell on his back as she landed on top of him. She was acting crazy— kicking, screaming, and scratching the camouflage-dressed man below her.

He quickly rolled over, pulled out a pistol from his right hip, and placed it to her head. "Detenlo ahora (*Stop it now*). Ahora (*Now*)!"

But she did not react to his order and kept flailing all over him. She was in such a trance of excitement, she clearly never saw the gun. The gun exploded into the left side of her head, and blood immediately blew out of her forehead on the right. She fell to the floor, lifeless. The man back-peddled on his buttocks away from the still body while pointing the gun at the rest of the awestruck passengers in the cabin doorway and then scurried up the stairway.

Frank couldn't believe what he had just witnessed. All were acutely without words. Helen and Soo Mi had their hands over their mouths as tears rolled down their cheeks. They grasped one another and held on.

Irving drooped his head and gave a glance up at Frank and Yuto. "Jesus, what the hell was that? I knew she was losing it, but, now, this surely has put us in one big pickle, for sure. They are not going to trust us at all from now on."

"My God, Irving, have you no heart? Kimberly was just murdered!" Helen said aggressively.

"I do have a heart, Helen. Kimberly has been losing it for some time now. I didn't send her out there. She did it herself. We all need to get home.

That's all I'm trying to do. I'm sorry if that makes you think I'm heartless," Irving said.

"Good she not in our plan," Yuto said softly.

Helen and Soo Mi looked at both men with disdain, but, deep inside themselves, they surely knew Kimberly was going to do something stupid, but, on the other hand, they had just witnessed her murder in cold blood.

As they all sat on their bunks, Frank had forgotten the door was still ajar.

Suddenly, the boss appeared at the door, his face red with anger, and he yelled, "How you say? Estupido, esa mujer (*Stupid, that woman*)!" as he pointed to the dead body behind him. "You no do again!" he barked and pulled his pistol from its holster and placed it on the side of his temple. "You do, and bang, bang! Entiéndeme (*Understand me*)?"

He moved forward into the cabin, and Irving stepped up to meet him. Before anyone could react, the boss lifted his rifle butt and smashed Irving across his face. He fell to his knees with his head bowed. The boss kicked him in the chest, and Irving's body flung backward. With one final motion, he grabbed the barrel of his gun and belted Irving's body three or four times for good measure.

"Entiéndeme (*Understand me*)?"

Yeah, I understand. You aren't long for this life, mi amigo. Now, I can live the life I want—killing. No more cutting up dead people. I'm going to enjoy this.

The boss slammed the door behind him then stomped up the stairs.

A few minutes later, one of his crew returned, opened the door, and without warning, threw a bucket in the cabin and shouted, "Sin baño para nadie (*No bathroom for anyone*). Poo poo en see cangilón (*Poo poo in the bucket*)!"

"They're pissed now. Christ Almighty. All of us pissing and shitting in a bucket. Goddamn it, Kimberly! Now we need a new plan," Frank said.

Helen and Soo Mi could only hang their heads as the men searched each other's eyes for ideas.

"We still have a plan. It is not lost. We need to be ready. We were caught off guard by that bastard and Kimberly. That will not happen again. Will it?" Irving asked, clearly not expecting an answer.

No one responded. They all looked at him and shook their heads. Everyone seemed to know that they were lost without Irving and his battle and special ops experience. He was their only hope, and it was imperative that they follow his orders.

~~ ~~ ~~

Kimberly's death had been unbelievably traumatic. The quickness of it all was incomprehensible to those who had never seen battle, guns, or fighting situations. As they laid in their bunks, Frank went over the details of the event leading to Kimberly's death. What could they have done to stop it? What could each have done to prevent Kimberly's depression? As time passed, Frank realized they could have done absolutely nothing to save her. What he *did* realize was their lives, too, were in danger, and their captives had no qualms with killing them if the situation warranted it. They were essentially pieces of meat, flesh dressed as humans, and to be sold to the highest bidder. They had no lives if this entire scene played out the way the captors wanted. They all had to do something. Waiting for servitude or death was their only option.

As if the captors wanted the passengers to know how evil they were, Kimberly's body was heard being dragged up the stairs, her head, going by the sounds, bouncing on each step until they reached the deck. Frank then faintly heard the straining of the guards as they must have lifted her body up and threw it over the side of the boat. The body seemed to land in the water just outside their cabin. Soo Mi sighed heavily, Helen cried, and the others bowed their heads. Irving sounded as though he was saying something in Hebrew, but Frank didn't understand what he said.

Night was nigh. The usual food for dinner was never served. No one came to the door. Their only solace was the bottles of water in the cabin. Dehydration certainly had to be avoided if these animals wanted to deliver their prey safely to others. Water was an absolute must, but, for now, food was being withdrawn as a punishment and a sign of things to come if they didn't heed their captives.

Just as Frank thought they were alone until morning, the key turned in the lock, and three men came in. Two of them stood at the door, and Hector pulled out some long, thick zip ties. He turned Frank around, grabbed his hands, and placed them behind him and tied them together tightly. He did the same with Yuto next and then Irving. He lined them up and motioned them to sit on one of the bunks, never speaking a word. He looked at the women who were cowering on the opposite bunk. Soo Mi was crying and shaking profusely, and Helen was trying to comfort her but sniffled as well. The pirate must have figured they were no threat, especially after they had seen what he and the others were capable of by killing Kimberly. He snickered and then brought out one more zip tie, grasped the right hand of Helen and Soo Mi's left hand, and tied the two women together. He revisited the zip ties of the men, checked the one on the women, glared around the cabin, and then gestured for the other two thugs to leave and exited the cabin. Again, one of them locked the door behind him.

~~ ~~ ~~

In the darkness of the cabin, Soo Mi daydreamed of the time when she was a child, being told of the deaths of her grandparents at the hands of evil people in their government. She could only imagine how they'd died, but she was told they were tied up and shot. Now, the reality of their deaths became crystal clear. After seeing how Kimberly's body had instantly stopped moving and became lifeless, she knew her grandparents never felt pain or fear of death by their executioners. She opened her eyes, stared at the bunk above her, and finally felt peace for them but fear for herself and her friends.

Chapter Thirty

Frank flopped onto his bunk, and in no time began that slow descent into a deep sleep where memories and fears were waiting.

Frank hurried to set the table for his bride and himself. He had their very own special wine ready to serve when she got home from shopping. She had thought he was taking her out for dinner since she had been so busy today. She seemed relieved this was happening. She said she couldn't stand to have to make dinner tonight. Frank had everything ready: appetizers, a main course of beef Stroganoff over rice, and her favorite dessert. He had even thought of the sorbet in a small glass to cleanse the palette between dinner and her tiramisu. The candles were placed perfectly on the table, and he had sprinkled rose petals on the white table cloth. He was 'The Man' tonight.

He hustled over to the oven to check he hadn't overcooked the appetizer, stirred it for a moment, then placed it back in the oven and turned down the heat. He was so excited as he went back to the table to pour the wine, glancing at his watch to see what time it was. Kate had told him to be ready as soon as she came home at six-thirty.

He ran over to the bay window of the living room to be sure she wasn't early and, not seeing her car, returned to the table to tidy up the tablecloth. No wrinkles for him. Everything had to be perfect. Then he heard a car entering the driveway. He hurried over to the window again, and there she was, getting out of the driver's side carrying some shopping bags.

She's gonna love this!

He looked through the window on the side of their front door, trying to see where she was so he could open the door as soon as she arrived in front of it. He timed it perfectly. He flung open the door, she looked up, he put his arms around her waist, and they kissed for a long time right there on the front stoop. She dropped her bags and threw her arms around his neck and held him there for even longer. He then picked up her bags, ushered her into the living room, sat her down, took off her shoes gently, and massaged her feet for her. Then he hurried over to the table and brought her a glass of wine and sat next to her with his, kissed her on the cheek, and said, "Dinner will be served whenever you want."

"We're not going out?" she asked.

"Nope, I've done it all for you."

"You shouldn't have…"

"Oh, yeah, I should have, for sure. Now drink up."

The dinner was a success if not an unexpected, wonderful surprise. They sat on the sofa, her head on his shoulder and her leg over his. Both slowly sipped their after-dinner drinks. Frank stroked her bulging tummy, lowered his head, and spoke adoringly to the little life within his wife's belly. He even sang a few bars of a lullaby he knew. The baby didn't move. He tried again and felt for the baby's movement, looked up at Kate, and she smiled. He felt again and again, tried pushing in a little to rouse the baby to move. It didn't.

Kate said, "Frank, I love you." She smiled again, totally at ease now.

Frank answered, "But the baby?"

"Never mind the baby, Frank. It's just us now."

Frank didn't understand. "What?"

Suddenly a gush of red fluid poured out with such a force, Kate's dress flew up and seemed to remain there forever as blood carried on flowing. The blood had pieces of white material within it and seemed to form an image of a gun. Frank pushed himself up and over her, only to see her smiling as the blood continued its course all over her dress, him, and the floor. He tried to hold Kate but couldn't. His hands were not there. He could see his arms but no hands!

He sprang to a sitting position, banging his head on the bunk above him. His eyes were wide and searching. "Kate? The baby?" he said.

Silence and darkness were all around him. There was no sofa, no after-dinner drinks, and no Kate. He laid back down on his bunk bed, tears rolling down his cheeks as he buried his head into his pillow. Sweat beaded out over his forehead.

Kate's losing the baby, and I can't help. Kate, please, think of me, keep me in your heart. I'm trying to get home. Hold on!

Chapter Thirty-One

Irving slid off his bunk above Frank, stumbled against the hull, and was able to finally rest on the edge of Frank's bunk. Both were encumbered badly by their zip ties. Neither one spoke as they desperately searched their minds for some solution to their situation.

"We will be coming to the rendezvous sometime, and we need to be ready to execute the original plan," said Irving.

"How? These damn zip ties are tight as hell. My hands are getting numb," Frank said.

"Yeah, me, too," Irving replied. "Let's wake everyone and see if we can find anything to snip these things."

"What about your knife?" Frank asked.

"I'm afraid that would dull the knife we need to cut one of the guard's throats. We can't afford to have a butter knife."

"Okay. Wait! I have something that we can use. My clippers!"

"What are you talking about? You daft?" Irving whispered.

"No, I have some nail clippers in my pocket. If I can wiggle my pants pocket over to your hands, you can get them out. They are in a little sac. I forgot they were there," Frank said.

Oh, my God, Kate. You saved me. You could be the reason for our escape and rescue!

"Wait a minute," Irving said, stopping Frank from turning himself. "Do you think those clippers will cut the ties?"

"Yeah, I think so. Even if they can't cut completely through, they can get a head start on us breaking free from them." Frank got up and peered out the porthole. It was pitch black. "It's still really early morning. Way past midnight for sure. I don't think the rendezvous is tonight. Don't you think we'd best try to commandeer this boat in the morning when they come for us? Let's wake the others."

Irving nodded, got up, and proceeded to wake Yuto as Frank shuffled over to Helen and Soo Mi.

When all of them were awake and sitting on the

bottom bunks, Irving said, "We're going to have to use our original plan."

"How, we no able to use hands!" Yuto asked.

"Frank has some clippers to cut the ties," Irving said.

Frank stood and said to Helen, "Use your left hand to get the sac out of this pocket."

"Which pocket, Frank?" she asked, scanning all the pockets of his cargo pants.

"The lower left pocket. It has a Velcro flap. Pull it up and get the sac."

Helen was able to retrieve the clippers, and she started snipping her tie to Soo Mi. The tie popped open. She immediately went over to Frank and cut his ties as Soo Mi moved over next to Yuto and hugged him. Soon, they were all free. Irving went over the plan again and again as explicitly as he had earlier. They all understood the absolute necessity of all of the plan working perfectly. Frank and Yuto looked at one another, clearly searching each other for any trepidation. They must have seen none. Both knew what they had to do. Everyone in the cabin had been emboldened by the purposeful murder of

Kimberly and the offensive way they had been treated and tied up. Their lives depended on them performing their plan quickly and precisely. Their fates were in their own hands.

"You guys ready?" Irving asked.

They all nodded. Frank knew the crew was ready mentally, but could they do it physically?

"Okay. I don't know what time it is or how many hours it will be before the goon or goons come, but I'm going to crouch by the door to hear them coming. When I tell you, get to your positions. Girls, get those strips of sheets ready to shove in the goon's mouth if he tries to scream out."

Helen and Soo Mi glanced at each other, gathered their strips together on their laps, sat on the edge of the lower bunks, and readied themselves for what may come.

And, then, they all waited.

Chapter Thirty-Two

A glint of sunlight shone on the floor of the cabin, heralding morning. Irving was still crouched by the door. The women were asleep, and the men were dozing off here and there. Irving got up and stretched from his hunched position that he had maintained most of the night. His motion roused Frank from his daydreaming, and Frank stood and moved to take Irving's place without saying a word. Irving nodded to say thanks and then laid down on the bed.

Yuto moved out of his way to allow him a restful position and then walked over and stood behind Frank as he huddled down with his ear on the door. Irving was soon asleep. His soft breathing then led to a whistling snore that was low-pitched, and all the passengers smiled, and Soo Mi giggled as he continued snoring.

It had been at least an hour since Frank had taken over the listening at the door. He hadn't heard any sounds of footsteps on the deck above. The pirates must be sleeping, and a sense of ease came over him. After several more hours, Irving woke with a start, eyes wide open, looking as though he felt fear until he recognized everyone in the cabin being somber but not excited.

"Shit, I've been asleep how long?" he asked.

"Don't know, three, maybe four hours," said Helen.

"Okay, I'll take over, Frank."

Frank thought maybe he should give Irving a bit more time to rest, but Irving moved so quickly to replace him, Frank felt obliged to stand up and get out of his way.

"Thanks," said Irving.

"Yeah, you okay?" Frank asked.

"Yeah," Irving remarked.

The hours again passed without Frank hearing much at all. The engines of the boat continued to hum along with no evidence of slowing. The sea was relatively calm, the sun shone brightly now, and the boat was not rocking side to side as it would if the waves were high.

"Why no hear anybody up there?" asked Soo Mi

as she pointed to the ceiling.

"I get the feeling they are preparing for the transfer. I'm guessing the boss is giving them their orders, being sure they're on the right course. I suspect the transfer has to be at night, you know, under darkness for fear of being seen," Irving said. "Frank, keep an eye out for sundown through that portal."

"Yeah, okay," Frank answered.

~~ ~~ ~~

It was now quite evident that they were all getting nervous about their plan, the execution of it, and the outcome of their lives if they screwed up. Irving said he knew it and went over the plan again, clearly trying to give them a feeling of strength and confidence. He discussed it with each of them, sat by their sides, and talked about the plan and what they would do to be successful.

Later, Irving suddenly rose from his crouching position and kneeled on one knee, waving his hand to the others. By now, they all knew this meant something's up and to be quiet. He then raised his hand with only his index finger showing.

Frank sighed with relief.

One goon! Thank God.

The crew stood still, awaiting any change in Irving's finger. His arm was still in the air when the middle finger went up.

Shit, two goons!

Irving stood with his ear still placed on the door. He moved his ear around several times, seemingly trying to find the best area to hear. He stopped and listened again. It was then that his middle finger flexed down, leaving only the index finger. Frank sensed the relief through the silence in the cabin.

Then Irving quickly pointed to the door with his index finger, alternating between pointing to the ceiling and pointing to the door as he fully stood up into a combative position.

"This is it, guys," Frank whispered.

The sound of a key entering the lock and turning was followed by the door slowly opening. Irving had been correct. There was only one pirate standing there with his AK-47 at the ready but relaxed, obviously expecting to find all of the captives still tied. The look on his face was that of not only surprise but horrible fear as Irving snatched the AK upright with his left hand, pulled him toward him into the doorway, and grabbed his shirt with his right hand. Irving let go of the rifle then jammed the base of his left palm into the base of the pirate's nose. Irving retracted his hand and struck the man in the throat with the side of his right hand. The man lunged for his throat. Irving spun the man around and positioned his hands on his head and neck, hyperextended his head, and twisted. The man dropped to the cabin floor. Irving quickly dragged his body into the room toward Yuto and Frank and closed the door.

Frank and Yuto took hold of the man, pinning him down. There were no muscular movements in response to their actions. Frank released his hold, as did Yuto. The man's chest remained motionless. Irving had killed him in very quick, adroit maneuvers just as he'd said he would. Irving dropped to the floor, removed the rifle from around his neck, and relieved the man of his pistol, handing it to Frank. Frank pulled the slide back a bit to check to see if there was a bullet in the chamber. There wasn't. He chucked the slide, loading a shell, then dropped the magazine to examine the number of shells in it. Irving got up and strode to the door to listen. Yuto knelt down and took out the two magazines from the man's belt and handed them to Frank as Yuto gestured for him to put them in his pockets.

"What next?" Yuto asked.

"Well, we have two options. Stay here and wait for the next goon to come and do the same thing or go up and face whatever comes our way," Irving replied.

"If we go up, there's no telling where they are or how we will be positioned to fight them. I vote to wait until the other comes down. We figured the boss was running the boat and Hector was his backup, leaving only one guy to come, right?" Frank said, looking to Irving for affirmation.

"Sounds like a plan," said Irving.

Again he crouched with his ear on the door, and they waited. Soo Mi shoved the man under the bunk and attempted to cover the opening under the bed with a blanket, but before doing so, she went through his pockets, keeping his switchblade knife and flashlight as well as some money. Helen looked surprised at her ingenuity and gave her a very congratulatory smile as she joined her in pushing the body well under the bunk.

They all then assumed their original spots for the next ambush.

Chapter Thirty-Three

A few minutes ticked off, and the passengers waited anxiously for the next confrontation, but no one came to the door. Frank wondered why. The boat was still churning away in the mildly choppy waters with no sign of slowing, so why did this goon come down if he was not going to get them ready for transfer?

"Carlos? ¿Qué estás haciendo allí abajo (*What are you doing down there*)? Hacer el amor con las mujeres (*Making love with women*)?"

Irving jumped up and, in a low but forceful voice, said, "It's time. They're looking for him!"

"Carlos? ¿Que esta pasando (*What's going on*)?"

"He wants to know what's going on with Carlos. I'm going to tell him everything is okay, all right?" Frank asked Irving.

"Sure, we have time," Irving responded.

"No hay problema aqui. Solo verificando a estos prisioneros y asegurándome de que estén bien amarrados para la transferencia," Frank uttered in a low, gruff voice, letting the other guy know he was just checking the ties and making sure things were ready for transfer.

"Bueno (*Good*). Darse prisa (*Hurry up*). Estaremos allí pronto (*We will be there soon*)," replied the other pirate.

"Próximamente (*Coming soon*). Solo algunas cosas más (*Just some more things*)," said Frank and then he whispered, "He says we're going to be there soon and to hurry up."

"Okay, we need to do this now," Irving said. "Tell the guy to come down and help. Uh, tell him one of the ties is tight and to get another one for him."

"Oye ven aquí. Trae a otro cremalleras. Estos son muy apretados. Demasiado dolor. Mal color en las manos," Frank said, telling the man the ties were too tight, giving pain, and cutting off the circulation.

"Bueno. Vengo," the man shouted.

"He's coming. Get ready!"

It's just like déjà vu all over again—just like Yogi Berra once said.

Frank was just so impressed at the skill, the cunning, and the quickness that Irving possessed to repeat almost the exact maneuvers he had performed on the other goon. Grab, pull, break a nose, and chop the throat of his victim, and then twisting him around like a rag doll, and, with one smooth motion, break his neck. It didn't even look difficult, but Frank knew the strength needed to execute the actions Irving had displayed was incredible, necessitating a well-trained and rehearsed muscle memory.

Yuto took no time to pounce on the second man, checking to see if he was still breathing. Suddenly, he reached for some of the sheet strips on the bunk and shoved them down the goon's throat. Soo Mi chimed in and pinched the guy's nose and sat on his forehead. The man tried to move his hands but began shuddering all over as his oxygen was diminishing quickly. Finally, Yuto motioned that he was definitely dead. The body was then stowed under the opposite bunk from the other and the opening covered with a blanket. His AK was taken, this time by Yuto; Soo Mi took the pistol and magazines, and Helen retrieved the large magazines for the AK and handed them to Yuto. Frank reached behind himself and slid the AK strap off his shoulder, held it out toward Irving, and nodded as if to say, "Here, take this. You'll need it." Irving grasped it and slung the rifle over his shoulder and across his chest so he could easily bring it up into a solid firing stance.

"Okay, we're halfway home here," Irving said. "The other two are probably busy getting ready for the transfer, but they are soon going to find out those guys are gone. I think it's time we start upstairs. I'll go first. Frank, you follow, then Soo Mi. Soo Mi, you know how to shoot that thing?"

"Yes, I take lessons one time but remember this 1911, nine millameta. I know how take safety off."

"When we start up, take the safety off." Irving took her gun and placed his right index finger pointing straight along the slide of the pistol. "Be sure your finger is like this. Only put it on the trigger when you have to shoot. Frank, Yuto, right? Yuto, you're after Soo Mi. Okay, Helen, you're last. Do you want a pistol?"

"No. Never shot one and I don't want to shoot you guys," she replied.

"All right then. Ready, folks?"

Everyone nodded with nervous affirmation. Irving opened the door, peeked out, and started up the stairs carefully and deliberately, step by step, waiting on each step for any unexpected noise or motion.

Chapter Thirty-Four

Just short of the top step to the next deck, Irving felt and heard the engines slow a bit. He squinted into the distance against the setting sun and thought he could see a tiny bit of land on the horizon. He wasn't sure, so he signaled his party to move down the steps until he could be certain they were nearing their destination or whether what he'd seen was an optical illusion. The boat then sped up and turned a little to the north and straightened out. Irving could tell that what he'd seen wasn't land. He had to coordinate his ambush with the boat nearing land so he could get his bearings. He decided to halt his ascent and motioned for everyone to return to the cabin.

"Damn," he said. "I thought I saw land when those engines slowed, but it wasn't. I need to see land. I think we will see some lights now that it is nearing nighttime, so you all stay here. I'm going up to the top step to keep watch. If one of them comes my way, I'll either take him out or get down here fast. Three knocks on the door means it's me."

They all quickly entered the cabin and closed the door. Irving positioned himself, hunched and peering over the top step, cautiously sticking his head out to see if he could find any signs of land.

And then waited.

~~ ~~ ~~

The sun was gone now, but no lights were visible. Irving figured it best to return to the cabin and wait there where he had reinforcements. He stepped back one step at a time, slowly, until reaching the floor in front of the cabin. With his back to the door, he rapped three times with his left hand. The door opened, and he slipped in.

"Someone count to six hundred. That will be close to ten minutes. I'll go up every ten minutes until I see lights on land. When I do, we will all go up together," he said.

"Do you know what the boss and Hector are doing?" asked Helen.

"No, but I'm guessing the boss has to be driving the boat. I have no idea what Hector is doing. It doesn't make sense that they haven't realized the other two haven't come back up, either. That can only mean that they are near the transfer site and are concentrating on being in the exact area at the exact time. Hector could be looking for light, too. Lights on land are our only hope to do our thing. I figure they will not be near a well-lit area, but even small towns have some glow of light like a halo at night, and as soon as I see any sign of that, we have to go. When we do, we go to the bridge in the center console. I'm figuring Hector is outside and the boss is inside. We have two AKs and two pistols, and they have two AKs and two pistols. We're even."

~~ ~~ ~~

Irving was once again hunched over in the stairwell at the top of the steps, hugging the left side of the wall to avoid being seen from that side where the bridge was located. He strained to peek over the side of the boat for light anywhere. He had a feeling someone else was looking as well. He just had to see it first. Suddenly, he saw a blink of light, but it didn't last long.

Was that a light?

As he elevated himself from his crouched position, he first checked his left side for motion. He stood up fully on the last step before the deck and scanned the lower aspect of the sky.

There it is again! Just a tiny blip. Is that really a light on shore?

He continued to stare and now saw several lights. He stood still to be sure these were lights from shore and not a boat. He figured a transfer boat would not have running lights at all. Any other boat would have them, but they would have some color to them to let other boats in the vicinity know of their position. He tensed up and tried to listen for any voices from the area of the bridge. He heard none.

They haven't seen the lights!

He squatted for a few seconds, closed his eyes, then opened them and blinked multiple times. Arising from the upper step, he scanned the ocean and again saw the two lights he had seen before. They were, indeed, small but close to one another. Once more, he switched from his eyes to his ears, listening for the boss' or Hector's voice.

Now's the time to do it!

He backed down the stairs until the bottom of the boat creaked. He knocked three times on the door. It opened. "Let's go. Just like I prepped you guys, okay?"

Just as he was about to ascend the stairs, the boat sped up, knocking him over the right side of the stairwell and almost sending Frank down the stairs. Soo Mi held Frank up. The boat swerved to the left and increased speed quickly. It had to be at top speed at this time. From the right and behind them, the sound of automatic fire started. Irving held his hand flat up and back at the others. He slid on his knees to the right of the entrance to the stairwell and looked behind their boat. There was another boat coming up quickly with no lights, but it was outlined by the multiple bright explosions from rifle fire from what Irving knew to be more AK-47s.

Rival pirates?

"More pirates trying to commandeer this boat," he said. "We can't take the boss out without slowing down and being captured and possibly killed. We'll have to wait to see the outcome."

"Shit," barked Yuto.

Soo Mi turned around in amazement. Hadn't she ever heard him say that word before?

"Everyone, get ready for a rough ride right here!" Irving ordered.

Everyone grabbed the railings on each side and tried to keep an even balance as the race between the two boats and the automatic firing continued.

~~ ~~ ~~

The boss was clearly getting as much speed out of his boat as possible, and it was working to his advantage. The other boat was keeping pace but it was not catching up. The boss glanced at his fuel gauge and wasn't happy with what he saw, for sure. He tried hailing Hector, who was trying to fire back at the pursuers. The boss was leaning out of the confines of the console bridge, one hand on the wheel and one hand banging on Hector's back.

Hector turned around, and the boss shouted, "Ve a la ametralladora ahora. Daré la vuelta al bote y los enfrentaré cuando estés listo."

~~ ~~ ~~

Frank translated the words in his head: *Go to the machine gun now. I'll go around the boat and face them when you're ready.*

Frank reached up and tapped Irving on his back and relayed his translation to him. Irving became wide-eyed in amazement at the words 'machine gun.'

Hector slung his AK over his shoulder and rushed forward toward the bow, an area none of the passengers ever saw or were allowed to go. He ripped off the canvas covering an armament, a Browning 191A4 thirty-caliber machine gun. He fed the belt of ammunition into the gun, pulled back on the firing mechanism, and loaded the first shell. This weapon was very prevalent in World War II and the Korean as well as Viet Nam War. What was good about it was the fact that it could be mounted almost anywhere, and here, the boss had it under wraps on the front of the boat as a precaution for just such an attack.

~~ ~~ ~~

"Tell everyone to keep down, get back in the cabin. This is gonna get crazy," Irving shouted.

The boat veered to the left and continued doing so until it had rotated almost one hundred eighty degrees. They were all slammed against the right side of the stairwell. Helen landed on the bottom floor while Yuto tried with all his strength to steady both Soo Mi and himself. The boat seemed to stall for a second and then went into high gear. Irving completely saw the entire turn and the other boat bearing down on the bow. He couldn't understand the boss' motives for such a stunt until he heard the enormous burst of automatic fire from the front of the vessel. The boat almost lit up with the explosions of the thirty-caliber shells, a sound he knew very well.

The attacking boat was not ready for such a massive barrage of firepower. The rounds were being poured out at well over two hundred and fifty per minute, and Irving knew the machine gun could fire at a faster pace, but he guessed they didn't have a lot of ammunition. Irving, Frank now beside him, saw the rounds hitting almost dead center of the attackers, each round heard and seen ricocheting off the metal tower and the hull of the now slowed attacker. The other pirates turned to escape the area, but, unfortunately for them, their decision was not a good one. As soon as they did, Hector powdered the side of their boat, and it soon became silent other than the idling of its motors. The boss reduced his speed to almost still, brought his boat close to the silent running vessel, and Hector once more blew out another burst, strafing the boat back and forth. Then the boss slowly moved to the other side and repeated the strafing. There was no response after that.

Frank looked at Irving as he just shook his head in amazement. The passengers were stooping down tightly in the stairwell. Soo Mi, Yuto, and Helen were unaware of what happened. They never had time to get to the cabin.

"Now's the time for us to get rid of this bastard," said Irving.

Knowing Hector was probably too busy

wrapping up things with the Browning, he aimed the group toward the bridge to take on the boss. They all hunkered down and moved silently.

"Carlos, Felipe.Ven aquí ahora. ¿Dónde estás?" screamed Hector.

Irving looked at Frank. "What?"

"He's looking for the other two."

Hector's quick footsteps pounded, him coming back while he ran from the bow on the right side of the console area. The passengers were on the left. They remained still and crouched as Hector rushed to the flight of steps to their cabin.

Irving turned to Yuto and Frank. "I'm after him. When you hear gunfire, take the boss and shoot him until he no longer moves, hear?"

~~ ~~ ~~

They nodded as Irving disappeared into the darkness back to the cabin. A moment later, gunshots, and they turned to go toward the bridge but were stunned by the presence of the boss standing just ten feet in front of them.

"Estás muerto, sabes (*You're dead, you know*).

You now muerto, mi amigos!"

He raised his AK and leveled it out as a grin revealed his brown, tobacco-stained teeth. The passengers froze knowing their fate. Then, two shots rang out. The boss just stood there, but no bullets or sounds came from his barrel. His knees buckled, his eyes bulged, and blood spurted from his right ear. The AK fell to the floor followed by the boss flat on his face. Behind him stood Helen with a pistol in her hand. Yuto instinctively reached behind himself to check for his gun he had put inside his belt and found it gone.

"You guys okay? I didn't hit any of you, did I?" Helen asked in a quivering voice.

Frank raced over to her, followed by the others. He took the gun from her still-shaking hand and put his arm around her as she slowly folded like a rag to the deck, sobbing. He held her there for a minute or so, then stood.

"Stay with her, Soo Mi," he said.

From there, Frank met Irving as he came back from dealing with Hector, and they proceeded to the bridge for anything that would help them. Frank found some maps seeming to be of the area they were in. Irving checked the fuel gauge and found it at a little less than a quarter of a tank.

He called for Yuto to come over. "You know what a siphon is?"

"No, what?"

"We need to get the fuel from the other boat into our boat. A tube that we can transfer the fuel from that boat to here," he said, pointing at the other boat.

"Oh, you want gas from bad boat?" Yuto asked. "Yes, I know now. Not know word, si..."

"Siphon?" Irving interrupted.

"Yes, I go look," Yuto replied and started back to the stern.

"You may have to look on the other boat. If you do, Irving or I need to go with you," Frank yelled as Yuto disappeared.

"We're drifting right now," Irving said. "Let's tie the other boat up in case we need their fuel, but only then. No telling if there are any people left over there. Here's west," Irving said, pointing out the compass on the dashboard. "That would be where

Brazil will be. We need to get to a well-lit city or big town and get to the police as soon as possible."

"Right," Frank agreed.

Yuto appeared a little later with not only a siphon tube but a sucking mechanism as well as a pump to facilitate the transfer. He also brought a long grappling hook if they needed to get to the other boat.

"I'd say you really do understand English a lot more than you put on," said Frank.

"Yes, understand better than talk," Yuto replied with a sheepish smile.

Irving picked up a flashlight and, with Frank and Yuto, went to the engines to find how to fill the tanks. Frank leaned over the side and extended the grappling pole, hooked it on to the bullet-ridden boat, and tied it off. He grabbed another area of the boat and pulled it alongside and tied it off as well.

Yuto hopped over the side and onto the crippled craft.

"Be careful. Wait for us," Irving shouted.

Once Irving was satisfied of the locations for fueling, he and Frank climbed over onto the boat where Yuto had remained. Frank had an AK, and the others had pistols. From there, Irving led them on a systematic search of the boat for anyone left alive, peering into nooks and crannies as well as cabins, radio rooms, and engine rooms. They found no one alive. Altogether, there were five dead bodies on deck. Yuto gathered up their armaments and magazines for safe keeping, saying he intended on taking them back to their vessel.

Irving searched the boat for its engines and the fueling locations, found them, and then instructed Yuto to go back and get the siphoning tube and accessories. Yuto dutifully picked up all the rifles, pistols, and magazines he could carry, climbed back over onto the boss' boat, and was gone.

"Jesus, that Browning machine gun was awesome. Wiped these poor bastards out clean and quick," Frank said, glancing at all the telltale bullet indentations on the boat and the multiple bloodied bodies.

"Yeah, these guys didn't have a chance. They had no idea what the boss had on his boat."

"Neither did we," Frank said.

~~ ~~ ~~

Yuto appeared with the siphon and had already placed his side of the tubing into one of the fuel pipes that Irving had left open. "Okay here. Sy...phone in here."

"Good job," Irving said, grabbing the other end and walking it back to the other engines. He set it up for the transfer. "First, I'll check and see how much they have." He disappeared to the bridge area. When he returned, he informed everyone, "They have more than we did, but it's not much more. Half a tank ain't bad, though. Of course, we don't know where we're going right now."

They finished up the transfer of fuel and took every bit of food and water left on board. Irving made one more pass around the boat, searching for anything that would benefit them, then climbed over the side back to their boat, untied the pirate boat, and let it drift away.

Once everyone was on board, they all went over to Helen, now sitting up but still comforted by Soo Mi.

"Quite a shooting exhibition, Helen. You saved us," Frank said and, turning to the others, he whispered, "Let's let her rest in the boss' cabin for now. I think we need to wait until dawn to get our bearings. No telling where we are in relationship to a big city. I know Rio is on the southern part of Brazil, but I think we are way up north if I can read this map right. We might not have enough gas to get to Rio."

"Let me see the map?" Irving asked, sliding it over to a larger flat surface. "This mark is probably where the transfer was to happen. It looks like we were quite far out northeast of there when I first saw the lights. I'm guessing we need to go south, if not southwest, but let's wait until morning."

"Sounds like a plan." Frank gestured with his thumb up. "We need a lookout while the rest of us sleep?"

"Not a bad idea. I'll take the first shift for an hour," Irving said while taking his watch off of the boss' right wrist. "I can now tell the exact time." Irving smiled and then sat in the captain's chair. "Get some sleep, folks."

The Mystery of Flight 2222

Chapter Thirty-Five

For once the passengers were able to sleep without fear or loss of hope. Frank woke with a feeling of energy he hadn't had in a long time. Each one had taken some time to stay as a lookout, and now it was about eight in the morning and everyone was milling around, especially Helen who said she was famished. She found the galley, cereal, coffee, juice, and some kind of meat that really didn't taste that bad. As to what animal it had belonged to, she had no idea.

She'd made the coffee and set out plates and eating utensils for everyone, and as they entered the eating area, she actually greeted them with a smile as if nothing ever happened the night before. Frank wondered a bit about that, but food and drink were the most important things on his mind today.

"Irving, do you know where we are?" Frank asked.

"Yeah, I was right. North of where we want to go. I think Natal is just south of here. It's a big city.

That will be our destination. I'm running the boat that way, I hope. The fuel gauge is now pretty good. We left the other boat with nothing to spare."

No one answered, all clearly being at ease with Irving's plans. They had an enormous amount of confidence that Irving would bring them to safety because they certainly had no experience to do it themselves, that was for sure. After breakfast, Soo Mi and Helen cleaned up their plates and then, as if on cue, they started cleaning up the entire mess hall and kitchen area. Frank had to laugh to himself because he knew Kate would have been doing the same thing.

Cleaning up the boat of some evil rotten pirates who would have killed us as soon as look at us? Yep, that's Kate, all right!

Later, each of the passengers came up on deck and stared at the horizon, searching for land or anything that would lead to the end of their ordeal. The ocean was calm, the sun shone brightly, and a small breeze was comforting. Irving was at the helm again, always studying the map on the console in front of him. It seemed as if he would never just sit back and relax, even now. He seemed to always be looking for something or improving on it. His ashen face was obviously a result of years of worry and deception, all the while attempting to appear at ease and calm.

Soo Mi and Yuto hung out together, sitting on the bow enjoying their respite and the warm sunshineon their faces. Frank arranged the rifles and the ammunition and took inventory of it all as Helen stayed away from the guns. She had never fired a gun or really ever held one that she could remember, so she'd said, until the night before. She'd also said that somehow, she hadn't come to terms with the murder of another human being, but she knew it was necessary for her life as well as the others, and she was at peace with that. However, in her mind, she felt there was no reason for her to relive the shooting of the boss by being close to the firearms at Frank's feet. She c alled out that she wanted to go over to Frank but she just couldn't do it.

Frank eased over to the hastily covered Browning on the bow. He was curious to see what kind of machine could have done all that damage on the pirates' boat. He loosened the tarp and let it drop to the base of the mount. He touched the barrel at its end and softly slid his hand down to the breech handle, pulled back a bit on the breech bolt, and part of a shell was visible.

Jesus, still loaded.

He eased the bolt back and then detached the belt of shells from it. He returned to the bolt handle, yanked back sharply, and ejected the shell. The noise of this large piece of ammunition hitting the deck jarred everyone's daydreaming. Once they saw the shell rolling on the deck harmlessly, they resumed what they were doing. Yuto left Soo Mi alone to examine the Browning.

"I never seen this in my life. It no shoot?" he asked.

"No more bullets. It's okay," Frank replied.

This destructive, massive piece of military hardware was so impressive, Yuto could barely stop touching it. He rubbed it and inspected every part as if he wanted to know everything about it. He then stood back and gazed in wonderment. "Most kill gun I know in my life," he finally said.

"Yeah, pretty impressive, I'd say, too," Frank said.

Irving then shouted, "There's another boat coming our way. Load that Browning again."

Frank hustled to reverse the unloading process as fast as he could. He fumbled with a couple of the shells on the deck trying to load the breech. He wasn't sure how to load it but figured it was the right way to get a shell in the chamber and then add the belt of shells second. Once he was ready, he swung the barrel to the west where there was a tiny dot of a boat speeding toward them.

"Everyone get a gun. This may be ugly," Irving yelled.

Frank sought desperately for the safety on the Browning since he was not familiar with it. He didn't even know if it had one. He figured that Hector had left it quickly, so he probably never put the safety on when he ran back to find the other goons. Frank finally found something he thought was the safety, but it was in the correct position for firing. He was ready but he was scared.

The boat coming from the west was joined by another. There was no question that one of them was going to go to the right of their boat and the other would go left. Frank became very nervous. He would be vulnerable no matter which way he fired. As the boats sped toward them and became larger and larger, it was apparent they were heavily outfitted police or military boats manned by many armed soldiers. Frank again rendered the Browning useless, threw the cover over it, and tied its rope around the base.

"Everyone! Unarm your weapons quickly. Put them all here on the bow. I'm stopping the boat. Line up on this side and put your hands up and behind your heads when they get near. Don't make any stupid moves to do anything from now on. It's going to be all right, but they don't know us from an enemy," Irving said loudly.

The military boats were much larger than their craft, and they almost engulfed it. The boats were maneuvered up against them, and soldiers jumped off and onto the deck where they quickly made the passengers kneel. The officers in charge then came on board.

"¿Quién eres tú (*Who are you*)?"

Frank took over the conversation and spoke fluent Spanish to the soldiers. He explained their plight from the beginning and even showed his wrinkled boarding pass to the officers, identifying him and the others as passengers from the ill-fated Air USA Flight 2222. One officer returned to his boat and radioed his information to shore, told the same story Frank had told him, and a response was heard, but Frank couldn't hear it well.

"You are an American?" one officer asked.

"Yes," Frank said.

"Your story checks out. We all thought everyone perished in the accident. You know that was fifty-two days ago?"

"Damn, lost count."

"Lucky, eh?" asked the officer.

"Yeah, really lucky, I guess. Wouldn't want to be that lucky again," Frank joked.

The Mystery of Flight 2222

Chapter Thirty-Six

The passengers were now safely aboard the military ships. They were told they were headed to Natal, a large city on the east coast of Brazil, in the state of Rio Grande do Norte. There, they were to be debriefed, their stories told, questions asked, and finally given good food and lodging. They would be flown to Rio de Janeiro and then home. All of this was being paid for by Air USA. Of course, there would be a large contingent of people awaiting them, including their families, friends, and the media. They would be billed as heroes and survivors. Their individual stories would be all over the news, books published, and probably some film company would produce a movie of their adventures.

Each one was overcome with emotion upon hearing they had come to the end of their horrid experience. Once they were by themselves, they reviewed each miserable day they had had over and over: the death of Maxine, Otto's heart attack, the ravaging death of Homer, the sharks, the flying fish that gave them life on the high seas, the murderous pirates who unmercifully killed Kimberly, the second bunch of thugs attacking them, and finally safety. They wanted to be sure that the story each would tell would be the same as the other's.

Frank desperately wanted to call Kate, but the people in charge told him they had contacted her through Air USA and let her know he was okay and gave her the information of his arrival home. They had relayed the fact that she was okay as well and would be waiting for him at the airport when he arrived.

They had all thought, without a shadow of a doubt, their fate was eventual death. None of them thought they would be in the arms of their loved ones or their families and friends ever again. They just couldn't wait to get on that plane to Rio and then home. It was such a warm and exhilarating feeling to know they would never have to go through this hellacious trauma again. Each of them cuddled up into a bed with clean sheets and soft pillows as they quickly fell asleep on terra firma.

~~ ~~ ~~

The next morning, they all received wakeup calls. Breakfast was served as room service with pancakes, eggs, papayas, coffee, yogurt, and pao frances, a small loaf of bread. An hour later, they were informed they would be leaving soon for the airport where the airlines had paid for them to shop for clothes and buy luggage for their trips home. Helen was especially excited about the luggage since her old raggedy suitcase was falling apart. And for all of them to be putting on new attire was going to feel so good after wearing the same clothes drenched with saltwater for fifty-two days.

They all convened in the lobby. There were cameramen, newsmen, and women everywhere asking questions in broken English and not really giving them time to answer. Yuto and Soo Mi appeared especially embarrassed to be so obviously inept in speaking English well, so Frank and Helen both simultaneously helped shield them from the media. Irving was his usual calm, demure self now. He gave curt, quick answers to questions but ignored many of them. They couldn't wait for the black SUVs to show up and whisk them away to the airport to go to Rio where they could shop. The flight to Rio was short and comfortable.

Once at the Rio de Janeiro airport, there were more media than at their hotel in Natal. Thankfully, the police were there to separate them from the adoring press and other onlookers. They were hustled into the local stores along the busy walkways until each found the luggage they wanted and then on to the clothing stores, dodging the throng of people following them with the help of the police.

At last, they were ushered into a large room far away from the maddening crowd where a lunch had been arranged and laid out for them. There was moqueca, a fish stew served in a clay pot, feijoada, coxinha, and a Gaucho rodizio, grilled meat off a skewer. An enticing pink drink, vitamina de abacate, was served. It was a blend of avocado, sugar, and milk. It was the same drink they'd originally had with the boss. The passengers had never eaten such a lunch and were absolutely 'filled to the gills' as Frank so plainly put it.

When their flight was announced, the airline representatives gave them all first-class tickets, and arrangements had been made that they all be boarded first and given time to get settled before others were allowed on, even the other first-class customers.

One by one they were welcomed on the plane by the airline crew and shown to their seats. Soo Mi and Yuto sat up front in the bulkhead seats on the right. Irving sat by himself behind them with a coat and tie on, a handkerchief in his coat pocket. Frank and Helen were in row three on the left. Frank offered Helen the window seat, but she turned it down. She sat after storing their belongings in the overhead bin.

One of the attendants came over and asked if they wanted anything to drink. Helen shook her head and said, "No," but Frank interrupted and ordered two Kaluhas and milk. Helen glanced quizzically over at him.

"For old time's sake." Frank smiled.

"With that enormous lunch and breakfast, I'm

gonna go to sleep before we get off the ground with that Kaluha," Helen said while yawning.

"I know how you feel. I think this may be the first time I go to sleep quickly on a flight."

He rang the attendant bell and asked for blankets and pillows. She brought two pillows each. Both of them plumped up the pillows and threw the blankets over themselves, and as true to their word, they finally gave in to their exhaustion and started to fall asleep with their tray tables down as a red-haired attendant placed their drinks in front of them.

~~ ~~ ~~

As they slept, other passengers boarded in the first-class area. One gray-haired woman with a plain, dark-gray dress, heavy brown stockings, and wide-heeled shoes wearing a 1930s type hat made her way to the seat in row two on the right. A very tall but huge, heavy-set man, who could just about make it down the aisle, was huffing and puffing from the long walk from the waiting area down the jetway to his seat next across from the old lady.

Then a scraggly looking young man arrived dragging a large duffle bag and tried to place it in an overhead bin. It was obviously not large enough to accept the bag, but he was resolute in trying. Eventually, an attendant came and informed him that his bag would need to be checked. He balked, continued to try for a while, and finally gave in. The attendant removed the bag from the area. He stared at her with disdain as she left, then he sat, pulling his hoody over his dirty-looking hair.

All passengers were soon boarded and seated. The usual safety video was shown on the screen of the Airbus 330 followed by the obligatory walk by of the attendants to be sure all seat belts had been fastened and all tray tables and seat backs were up.

"Attendants, please prepare for take-off."

The usual silence in the cabin occurred with this statement.

The 330 taxied onto the runway and made its way behind a jumbo 747. It was seventh in line to take off. Inside the cockpit, Captains Swanson, first officer Crenshaw, and second officer Hodges were performing their final check and recheck of all systems. Everything was right for take-off. The giant engines then raised their decibel levels to a high roaring pitch as the 330 increased speed down the runway to enter the evening sky. The last irregular clatter of the plane against the tarmac disappeared, the whirring of the landing gears entering their compartments with a clunk was heard, and a residual thrumming underneath finally stopped, allowing no more evidence of take-off but a calming hum, the only sound remaining in the cabin.

~~ ~~ ~~

Helen and Frank had slept through the take-off, and both woke at the same time and were surprised to see the drinks in front of them. Frank thought it a bit creepy that his favorite drink was in front of him as well as the woman next to him, but, still feeling sleepy, he dismissed the thought and proceeded to imbibe with his seat partner. The ice in the Kaluhas had melted a bit, but both took sips from their glasses, eventually finishing them.

"Good evening, ladies and gentlemen. Welcome to Flight 2222. We have now leveled off at thirty-seven thousand. Our flight time to New York will be ten hours and thirty-six minutes. The weather seems to be very nice for the first part of the trip, but after passing the equator, we may have some turbulence, possibly some mild stormy weather. This is not unusual on this run. We will keep you informed of our progress as we get nearer to our destination. Now, please sit back and enjoy your meals and entertainment. Thank you for flying Air USA."

Helen hung on every word. Frank noted her reaction and smiled at her.

"A heck of a mouthful, eh?" Frank said.

"Yeah, it's hard to believe we are five miles above the earth."

"Actually, six-point-nine miles. And we are still breathing," Frank jested.

"Whatever. We're really way up here, aren't we?"

"Yes. You know there is a group of people who believe that planes are not able to fly whatsoever?"

"Really? How's that?"

"Well, they think there's a movie being shown

on a screen outside each window, giving the impression that one is flying, and somehow the plane is being juggled around and noises made to convince the passengers they are flying," Frank replied.

"You're kidding me, right? What do they think when they are in another city when they land?"

"I guess they haven't figured that out yet." He laughed.

Helen let out a laugh, too, and seemed more relaxed in her seat. Frank ended the conversation and pulled out his newspaper. To be sure she was okay, he glanced over at her as she turned toward him.

~~ ~~ ~~

"So, what brings you to Argentina?" he asked.

"A family matter."

"Yeah, you got family there?"

"So to speak. A death in the family," she replied

"Sorry to hear that. I'm Frank. You?"

"Oh, Helen. Helen Hampton," she said, turning toward him.

"Hampton doesn't sound Argentinian."

Helen clearly waited for him to continue on. Frank was speechless for a second or two, expecting her to speak. "Uh, Mason, Frank Mason," he replied, somewhat embarrassed that he didn't tell her his last name right away.

"Doesn't sound Spanish, either." Helen giggled.

They both laughed, and each took a sip from their cups.

"Excuse my prying, but I can see you are a bit nervous on a plane," Frank said.

"That would be an understatement. I haven't flown a lot, but I have flown, and it is always tough for me," she answered.

"Well, let me give you a few facts to allay your fears. First, flying is actually the safest mode of transportation. In fact, the odds of a plane crash are one for every one-point-two million flights, with odds of dying one in eleven million. Your chances of dying in a car or traffic accident are one in five thousand. Did you know a plane is safer than a train?"

"My, my, you do know something about planes."

~~ ~~ ~~

"On another subject, I have a game I play on these long trips. It helps spend the time and challenges your thinking powers. Want to play along?"

"Another bunch of plane trivia?

"Nope!"

"What's that then?" she asked.

"I pick out seven people and try to figure how old they are, what nationality they are, what kind of job they have, what their names are and whether they are married or not, and anything else I can think of."

"Why seven?" she asked.

"Gosh, I have no idea. It has always been seven, I guess. No reason."

"Okay, begin with jerko over there." She laughed, pointing at the scraggly hippy.

"Well, he is definitely single," Frank blurted, almost spitting out his drink.

Helen leaned forward in convulsive laughter,

spilling her drink on her dress. Still chuckling, she wiped her skirt with her napkin. "Duh!" she finally whispered. "Don't do that again. That was funny."

"Hey, it's got to be true, right?"

"Yup. What else?" she asked, becoming more excited about the game. "Of course, there could have been another flower child who was stupid enough to marry this wanker, and it lasted two or three weeks."

"Now you're getting into the game. He's probably part Greek and part Irish. He has to be a busboy somewhere. He can't have the smarts to be anything but. Ah, let's see. His name is...Homer," Frank said, placing his thumb and index finger on his chin.

"No way. He's a Herbert. That's why he is so angry. He's had that hanging over him all his life. So he's miserable. I think he's a student. Probably all C's in his junior year. Community college, though, works part time as a computer programmer. The other part is spent teeing people off," she replied.

"Really? A brain, has he? Come on! Let's get real. Oh, we're really close on this one," Frank responded, raising his eyebrows. "This idiot has to be doing some cubicle job where he relates to no one but himself. He probably never communicates with real people in his job. His inner self is the center of his world. A hamburger flipper named, ah, okay, Homer!"

"Well, I have to agree with you there. I'd like to smack him upside the head and straighten him out. Who's next?" Helen asked, sitting up higher to choose someone.

Her remark was somewhat surprising to Frank. He didn't think she was so adamant about this jerk's actions, but it was obvious she was much more turned off by them than he was, and he was really disgusted by him.

"How about that gentleman with the coat and tie on, handkerchief in his coat pocket?" Frank suggested.

"Oh, that's too easy," she said confidently.

"Excuse me, what would you like for dinner? We are serving beef or chicken," an attendant interrupted.

She was a redhead with a short haircut, slender

to the point of being skinny, but with a pleasant smile and manner about her. Frank noticed the name, Kimberly, on her brass tag pinned to her blue and white Air USA blouse.

~~ ~~ ~~

"You rang?" another attendant asked. She was older and more seasoned than Kimberly. Her demeanor was all professional. No smile, no specific eye contact.

"Please, two Kaluhas and milks on the rocks here."

"Sure, that will be twelve dollars. And I'll be back in a minute with the drinks."

They sipped their drinks in silence, both of them checking out who they would choose next as their choice in Frank's game. He continued to suck on the ice at the bottom of his glass container, trying to get every bit out of his six dollars as he watched the movie progress without sound.

He turned and raised his head to scan the nearby passengers to begin the guessing game again but found Helen fast asleep, the headset cockeyed across her forehead.

Sleep tight, little lady. Wish I could sleep on a flight. We can continue the game later.

Frank stretched out his arms in front of him and suddenly was overcome by an enormous yawn. Evidently, all the excitement, food, alcohol, and the long day behind him would allow him to sleep on a plane for once. He leaned back, grabbed a pillow, drew the blanket up over him, and fell fast asleep.

Chapter Thirty-Seven

"Everyone, fasten all seat belts, we have no left engine, we will need to ditch into the sea. FASTEN SEAT BELTS! ASSUME CRASH POSITIONS!" a voice bellowed over the intercom system.

The attendants were scurrying up and down the aisle, awakening passengers who did not respond to the orders. Other passengers had been aware of the sudden explosive sound and subsequent severe rattling and tilting of the aircraft. Screams and audible, fearful voices were increasing in intensity as passengers grasped desperately at the seats in front of them, heads darting every which way to see what others were doing.

"Helen, Frank, wake up. Be sure your seatbelts are on and tight," Kimberly said to Frank. "We are having tremendous problems right now, be alert. Assume your crash positions. An engine's on fire. We're losing altitude, and we're crash-landing into the sea." Kimberly was shaking Helen and prodding Frank and forcefully speaking to them. "Hurry up!"

~~ ~~ ~~

Frank's sleep fog evaporated immediately, and they followed her instructions. As Frank leaned over, the early brim of the rising sun beamed through Frank's window, illuminating Helen's terrified face screaming without outward sounds.

Frank sat upright in his seat, glanced at Helen as she was grabbing his right hand with her right hand, and trying to stuff her left hand into his belt. He loosened his belt so she could get a better hold and then tightened it through a natural instinct. As he peered above the seats in front of him, he saw the game players: Kimberly, Maxine, Otto, Homer, Soo Mi, Yuto, and Irving, all staring back at him with dejected déjà vu expressions on their faces.

"Damn it! Here we go again. See you guys on the raft," Frank shouted as they all fastened their seat belts, leaned over, and ducked their heads.

Epilogue

You can't tell a book by its cover, and you can't trust this author and his characters, either.

You are now aware that Frank and Helen and their fellow survivors are caught in a repetitive dream of agony, death, cannibalism, fear, and temporary escapes only to be forced to live that same reverie again and again. What you may not realize is that they were specifically chosen to have their lives placed on hold while they continuously undergo the torment of this collective nightmare.

You see, their dastardly behaviors of the past are the key to their miserable dilemma. Yes, even though they appear to be either normal or slightly dysfunctional people, they all have a very dark side—a life no one ever sees, a life unbeknownst to even their closest relative. It is for these purposeful and often evil indiscretions that these nine individuals have been chosen to endure the anguish of a repetitive, heinous, sleep adventure. They are being punished for their evil, deceptive, and often deranged actions against others and society.

~~ ~~ ~~

Maxine has always presented herself as a matriarch, someone whose life has been spent serving others and obtaining a high stature wherever she went, but that is not the case. Maxine actually spent her life casting her 'sweet' demeanor in front of her as a shield to hide her inner hatred for the people around her. As a child, she *was* sweet, innocent, and unassuming, but as she grew into her teenage years, she found that there were much more rewarding ways to get what one wanted than being nice. She often stole small insignificant items from other students, not that she really wanted them, but she relished their sadness. She hoarded their items and used them as gifts to encourage the recipients to respect and love her.

She hated being forced to take piano lessons, and, instead of quitting, she launched herself to becoming proficient at it, knowing full well she could use this talent to destroy others. She especially loved to excite young aspiring pianists by building up their confidence and then tearing them down just when they thought they had succeeded. She would do so in the most innocent and seemingly benevolent ways, usually by overextending their abilities through advanced music for which they were never ready, all the while spurring on her intense dislike and jealousy for the children. The parents ultimately felt the fault was with their child's incompetence, not their teacher.

She honed her skills as a teenager and in her young adult years, and as she saw her own success, others suffered. These successes emboldened her even more when she applied for jobs where she could embezzle large amounts of money, hoard the cash, and then launder it so no one was the wiser. She was so good at it, no agency she worked for ever suspected this 'sweet' woman as a deplorable employee. Once she felt she was close to being identified, she would promptly offer an excuse to tender her resignation and find employment elsewhere. Her previous employer would always write a glowing referral letter for her, a fact that amused Maxine tremendously.

She had stolen from multiple companies and organizations, and, in fact, created a large nest egg for her retirement, but her thirst for her criminal activities drove her to distraction. She just had to shoplift, stealthily abscond with her friends' credit cards, and scam others on the internet. It was a nasty habit, but it had become an exciting part of her existence, and she couldn't live without ruining someone's day or life.

She eventually sought a small town to live out her days. She was the resident piano teacher and church-goer who everyone adored. She was asked to participate on their school board, and with the knowledge of accounting, to be responsible for their books. She reveled in being appointed to the church and school board's accounting positions since there was no one else to whom she was accountable. She was quite comfortable financially before moving to this town, so her embezzlements were small and almost imperceptible. This was the way she wanted it. She had been diagnosed with cancer that had spread and didn't have the mental or physical energy to put into planning new strategies. She dreaded intravenous chemotherapy and the sickness it created. She opted for oral medications because she wasn't in terrible pain. When it dawned on her that her life was to be over soon, she thought she would take one of the few vacations she'd ever had, to Argentina. Why Argentina? She did not know so she made up a reason.

True to her deceitful nature, she somehow persuaded the town's people to feel beholden to her and surreptitiously donate their hard-earned cash to pay for the trip, her last scam.

For living such a life of antipathy, loathing, and deceit, Maxine was chosen to be on Flight 2222 to Argentina.

~~ ~~ ~~

Otto was born in the poorest of neighborhoods. His father was a hard-working man trying to make ends meet, but his mother couldn't resist harassing him for his measly paycheck. He was a mountain of a man, strong and powerful in his appearance. His wife's continued intimidation forced him to seek income elsewhere. He was totally against stealing as he was brought up as a religious man and felt guilty even thinking about taking what others had. However, times were hard on him, and just when he thought he could no longer afford to be shackled as a father, he was offered a job by a recruiter from the local crime syndicate.

He was instructed to go to certain local establishments, walk in, mention the boss' name, receive an envelope, and return them all to an office at the end of the day. In the beginning, his job was 'temporary' and not full time, so he had to continue working his shift. He didn't know what was in the envelope. The owners were very nice and accommodating, so he thought nothing of it. The job paid a heck of a lot more than he was capable of getting anywhere else. He was soon taken on full time, and as Otto grew up, his father used to take him along with him to 'work.' Otto loved going with his father, meeting people and being given candy and cakes as he stood by him while the envelope was passed to his dad.

One day when Otto was thirteen, his father was sick, and Otto was told to go to the shops he knew well and pick up the envelopes and bring them home. His father's sickness was prolonged, and Otto eventually took over for him; however, he was not like his 'old man.' He was even bigger and more powerful-looking. He had a mean disposition about him. His presence was, in fact, awe-inspiring, but not in a good way. The proprietors were terribly afraid of him, even though he never threatened them.

Otto got used to this type of reaction from people. He loved how they cowered when he approached. He spoke softly, but if he saw any inkling that he was losing his advantage, his disposition visibly changed, and the person he was addressing would instantly know he was not to be fooled with.

As time went on, the bosses included him in more serious jobs that included risky and precarious situations. He soon realized how much higher up in the organization he had become and how he now had to use physical strength to enforce his intentions. He became a highly dangerous man to be reckoned with. People went out of their way to avoid him, and if they couldn't, they would give him anything he desired. The bosses loved Otto, and he was promoted almost yearly to positions of power.

Money was never an issue. He was well-paid both by his seniors and other people who wanted him on their side. Mayhem, chaos, fights, maiming others, and even being an accomplice to murder were part of his life, and he was loving it. He took advantage of everyone he could. Money was his only love. He never remarried after his first marriage failed miserably; however, he did have a family as a result—three sons who were estranged. Memories of his mother browbeating his father bothered him tremendously, so he could not risk marrying again and finding out his wife was like his mother again.

Eventually, having achieved one of the highest echelons of the organization, he was no longer physically responsible for the orders he was given. He could relegate them to others lower than he. It was more relaxing and comforting to Otto to know he would be behind the scenes rather than up on the front lines where he could be arrested, prosecuted, and thrown in jail for years. He had successfully avoided all of that, so there was no need to prove his worth anymore.

As a result, Otto essentially sat behind a desk and barked out orders. He ate breakfast, went to work, ate lunch, went back to his office, talked on the telephone, and put out an occasional fire. At the end of the day, he again ate at local restaurants where he was treated as a king—double helpings of food, wine, liquor, cigars, and anything else with which the owners could butter him up. Women 'adored' him or had to adore him, and he availed himself of their sexual advances often. Eventually, he was given permission to open a bar, essentially distancing himself from the organization without totally eliminating his job. Otto jumped at the chance and did well in that business. His reputation did help bring others into his 'Big Guy' bar, and he knew it and charged people for the right to do so.

His once intimidating, powerful size became an enormous bulging body of flab. His clothes were custom-made. None could be found in department or men's stores in the city. He was driven everywhere, rarely walked up or down stairs, and always used the elevator. His office desk chair was discarded and replaced with a wide double sofa chair that was elevated on blocks so he could reach the items on the desk. His enormous size was becoming a health detriment, and he knew it. Diets never worked. He had absolutely no willpower to deal with the diet restrictions placed upon him. He lived to eat, not eating to live. Owning a bar and taking liberty with the food and booze didn't help, either.

His plight was ultimately recognized by his peers and those higher up. He was invited to a meeting where all of this was presented to him. He was thanked profusely for the decades he had put in, rising from a lackey to one of the most powerful, but his journey had come to an end. He was to be put out to pasture, so to speak. It was really not unexpected, but he had one request. He did not want to be embarrassed and forgotten in the town in which he had grown up. He wanted to get out of America and see the world before it became so physically impossible he couldn't move. As a retirement gift, the organization paid for him to travel the world, knowing full well he would never be bothered by the syndicate. He opted to go to Argentina to start his new journey.

And so, Otto was also chosen as a passenger on Air USA Flight 2222.

~~ ~~ ~~

As you already know, Homer was mean, detestable, and ornery. His life had been a mess, but what you don't know is his overall addiction. It is not an addiction to drugs. Oh, sure, he smoked marijuana and dabbled in higher drugs such as crack. He was smart enough to stay away from heroin. He never liked the idea of needles. As a kid he was terrified by the vaccination shots for diphtheria, measles, and pertussis. He'd fainted a few times as a teenager when receiving a tetanus shot after cutting himself on a rusty object. He never remembered when he got the last shot, so when asked, he couldn't tell the nurses or doctors. Then, he would have to get another. It was pure torture just to see a needle, so it wasn't any problem to avoid shooting up even when his friends pressured him.

His addiction wasn't with alcohol, either. In fact, he despised people who were drinkers. He abhorred the drunks he'd see stumbling out of bars or laying prostrate on the ground. He often wished those 'dead drunk' people were really dead. What use were they to anybody? Of what use were they to the world? He actually found it difficult to even drink a beer. If he was hot enough—'dripping sweat' hot enough, that is—he enjoyed an ice-cold beer, but only one. He could not understand drinking bottle after bottle of beer just to drink it. It made no sense to him, and when others did, they either got obnoxiously funny or terribly mean and combative. He hated them.

No, Homer's addiction was arson. Fire had captivated him ever since watching his mother smoke. He used to take her matchbooks, hide in the cellar, and light one after the other just to see the flame. Staring at the flame allowed him to enter another world. The yellow center and the blue halo that would come and go at the end of the match were invigorating. What he loved the most was matchsticks. Their flame lasted for a while because they were long and thicker. He thought the colors were more brilliant that those from the flimsy thin paper ones. Then he was introduced to lighters. "What an enlightenment," he would say when he first rotated the rough circular wheel against the flint. He loved to see the spark grow into a beautiful flame that would last just as long as he wanted.

It was soon after that he started lighting things on fire. He knew the dangers of fire; therefore, he never lit anything in his room or his house for that matter. He would go into the backyards of other homes, clean out areas of debris, leaves, and any trash. Sitting on the dirt, he lit small pieces of paper he found in the rubble he had cleaned away. Ultimately, the things he lit were larger and larger, and his sickness became a true addiction. He never thought of those people whose lives he destroyed when lighting garages and then homes and watching them burn to the ground in the distance. He would time the fire department's arrivals and keep a journal of their times of response and the time it took to battle and put out the blaze.

He knew this was a real mental problem and he had actually studied what made people pyromaniacs. He liked the word but felt the word 'torch' was better suited to him. Studies had revealed that most people like himself set fires for self-gratification or as a release of tension from their daily lives. His tension was from his entire life, especially flipping burgers with other ne'er-do-wells. He knew some pyromaniacs were paranoid and psychotic, but he did not lump himself in their category at all. After all, he was not insane, he just liked fire.

He never made a concerted effort to expand his knowledge of fuels, which items burned the fastest, which ones burned the hottest or other more esoteric categories. He knew the object to set ablaze needed lots of air and sufficient fuel to get the job done. There was no reason to use some complicated method to start the fire, such as some remote igniting device used from afar, just enough fuel and a good, long-lasting flame. Then, all he had to do was find a floor or deck next to a flammable wall. Sheetrock walls did not burn well. He wanted the fire to start with wood paneling and in a room with sofas and chairs of wood. Once he could see it was proceeding, he could leave the premises and know it would go well.

Overall, Homer did not think he ever killed anyone in his fires. Granted, he didn't stay around too long to find out, but he did read the papers the next several days after and tried to follow the story. To his knowledge, he never read about anyone dying because of his actions. This made him feel better about himself.

On his last arson, he chose a bigger building than the small homes he had been using. It was his workplace, the burger place. He hated the manager and some of his fellow employees, and his anxiety was at its highest when he left every night. The problem was, he had brick and cinderblock to work with rather than a wood structure, necessitating more fuel and being there longer. He thought he had been identified by some people who happened to be around the back of the building just after he lit the fire, so he gathered up some belongings in an old duffle bag and decided to leave the country. He had never thought where he would go. Argentina just popped into his mind, so he tried booking a flight the next day.

Air USA, luckily, had one seat left on Flight 2222.

~~ ~~ ~~

Kimberly's background had only been covered superficially earlier with her relationship with Alice and Dave. Trusting anyone getting close to her was something she desperately wanted but never seemed to accept due to her psyche self within. She was hardheaded, for sure. This trait became evident when she was barely a teenager. In school, she was bullied, sometimes unmercifully by a group of girls who thought they were the most beautiful, talented, and smart. Kimberly initially did not fight back, figuring they would eventually leave her alone, but that didn't happen. It only got worse. One of the girls, unknown to the others, befriended her once in a mall where they both were shopping while their parents waited for them. She seemed so honest and forthright in wanting to be her friend. Subsequently, this girl, Stephanie, secretly met with Kimberly, and they developed a close relationship, sharing their most deep and personal thoughts, feelings, and secrets. Kimberly felt a special bond existed between them.

After a while, Steph asked her if she would come to a meeting where she would introduce her to the group of girls she was a part of, the ones who'd once bullied her. Kimberly had not been bothered by them ever since striking up a rapport with Steph. She felt that Steph would be her liaison into the group and that her life was going to be so much better from then on. At the meeting, Kimberly was welcomed and hugged and thoroughly accepted; at least, that's what she thought. Suddenly, things changed, and the other girls started snickering and laughing as they presented a slide show of Kimberly's life with photos and quotes. The photos were taken with her partially undressed by Steph in her home while they were exploring each other's bodies. The quotes were words she had never said to anyone in her life other than Steph. The entire time she was being humiliated, Steph stood by the projector and laughed and giggled. She replayed the photos and spoke the words of Kimberly's quotes repetitively. Kimberly was utterly disgraced in front of her peers. She felt shame like she never had before and ran from the room in tears.

For weeks thereafter, she plotted her revenge. It all started with simply slashing the tires of those girls' bikes, all lined up and locked in place at the school. Then, she poured liquid soap into their water bottles and spread red glitter in their lockers with a syringe. She made posters which said: Having a Bad Day? Call this number and take it out on me!

Of course, the number was that of each girl of the group who had been present at her humiliation. She soon added to the poster: Because I'm a spoiled brat bully and deserve it. Prank calls welcome!

At the bottom of the poster were their numbers in tear-off sheets like the advertisements one sees in grocery stores or the post office.

These antics worked but did not satisfy her obsession to repay those girls for their actions. She stepped up her game over the next year or two by growing into a good-looking woman, appearing older than her age. She had a lovely figure and started to use her new-found physical traits to bolster her reprisals. She flirted with their boyfriends, absolutely intent on breaking up the relationships. She offered the boys oral sex to woo them away from them. She was able to set up a camera in the girls' locker room and took naked pictures of them and placed them all over the school and the internet, some of which went viral. Still being consumed with anger, she actually hired people to harass her 'enemies.' She told them what to do and where to do it, and then she waited in hiding to watch it all happen.

All of this culminated one day when one of the girls committed suicide. Kimberly did not believe her actions caused her to take her life. The girl had had other mental issues, but deep in her mind, Kimberly felt relief that her vengeful activities in the past were part of her demise. Since that time, anyone who crossed her was a target of her twisted mindset; however, all of this was wearing her down mentally as well.

After graduation, this obsession continued in other ways. The girls who'd started it all had disappeared from her life. She became a loner but still tried to entice women and men into relationships and then purposely attempted to damage them psychologically if they strayed from her desires. This was why she opted to become a flight attendant, believing she would be traveling a lot and her abilities to avoid relationships would be enhanced, and she could escape the enclosed world she had built around herself.

Her assignment to Argentina just happened to be on the same day of the other eight passengers, Air USA Flight 2222.

~~ ~~ ~~

Soo Mi's and Yuto's confession to the group on the day Helen divulged her life was not the entire story, either. They both had lied. Yuto and Soo Mi were radicals in the making, even when they were children. Yuto could not stand the pomp and strict Japanese traditions. He felt they were all outmoded, archaic, and ridiculous. He rebelled against them most of his life, although he often had to give in to them but not without a fight. His parents were at their wit's end most of his childhood and teenage years. He hated going to their religious temples and shrines. His parents were of the Shinto culture where they worshipped in the dwellings of Kami, the Shinto gods. There were many sacred objects stored there that are not seen by anybody. They mostly went there to pay their respects and to pray for good fortune. Yuto could not understand hiding away objects to never be seen by anyone, and to pay respects to these without seeing them made no sense. There were so many times he laughed at the Komainu, a pair of guardian dogs on each side of the temple entrance. He mocked the purification troughs where participants washed their hands and mouths before approaching the main hall. Yuto once dipped his feet in the trough to the horror of others.

His disdain for the Shinto religious culture drove him to Catholicism where he eventually became a Christian. He did this more to punish his parents than believing in God in the beginning. He relished their unhappiness, feeling they deserved it as they had forced Shinto on him. He felt more at ease in the Catholic Church, but again the traditions and rituals bugged him so much he lost interest but maintained his desire to believe in God and Jesus. Granted, he did not really follow or pay attention to the Ten Commandments for he made his parents' lives pure hell.

Soo Mi had essentially the same type of background, but she was more outrageous about it. She physically lashed out at her parents. They were Buddhists. Scholarly studies were encouraged when she was young, and meditation and mindfulness to fulfill their lives were always emphasized. Soo Mi would have none of this. She often ran away, only to be found by her family and brought home to endure the horrors of their traditions and rituals. She didn't care whether people suffered as Buddha had, and, in fact, adopted the three poisons for suffering—Desire, Ignorance, and Hatred—rather than avoiding them. She joined every radical group she could as she grew older and participated in many heinous attacks on religious structures and their representatives.

She met Yuto by chance and was quickly drawn to his philosophy of life as he was to hers. They tormented their parents when they split from their families to escape them. On top of everything, they told their parents they had married just to plunge the final dagger of hate into their hearts because they both had been told all their lives never to marry outside their ethnic walls. This one action made them love each other more and more, and they both told each other they would rather die than be separated.

They both left their pasts behind them, flew to America to see the sights they had only seen on videos and movies, and, as a surprise, Yuto arranged a trip to Argentina for both of them on Air USA Flight 2222.

~~ ~~ ~~

Irving Kaplan was indeed in the Israeli army and was a member of the Special Forces, Shayetet 13; however, his life before joining was nothing like the other eight passengers. His childhood was happy, comfortable, and surrounded by a loving mother and father and multiple siblings. They all spent time together, each loving every minute of it. Even when the children became teenagers, ready to explore life and rebel a little against authority, they didn't. They were not afraid to do so, but the happiness of their lives and the satisfying wellness they all felt was the adhesive that bonded them.

Nothing personified his family more than his thirteenth year of life and his Bar Mitzvah. As a Jew, a boy becomes a man at this age. He is ethically and morally responsible for his actions and decisions. Most people think the bar mitzvah is the celebration after his ceremony, and it has become such, but, in actuality, at the age of thirteen, the boy becomes a bar mitzvah. Irving often remembered this time reverently and how proud his parents and entire family were that day.

At the age of eighteen, it had been decreed by the Israeli Defense Service Law that all Israelis were conscripted into the army at this age through to their twenty-sixth year, for thirty-six months, except women, who are required to do so for twenty-four months. Irving felt a great patriotic duty to join despite the mandate; however, his training caused him to change from a loving boy with family and friends to a man who was preoccupied with being the best of the best. He threw himself into his training programs much more than the average soldier and succeeded in everything he did.

Unfortunately, his obsession became derailed slowly to the point where strategizing to attack, defend, maim, and kill were consuming his attention daily. When, finally, he was in combat, he found the actions of shooting to kill or hand-to-hand fighting were primary instinctive actions, and his superior officers were watching. His decision-making was poor. He never disregarded orders or avoided doing what he was told, but his commanders often overlooked his promotions based on his being a 'loose cannon' at times.

As a result, his desire to become the best and exceed the expectations of his superiors were deflated, and he became more secluded as an individual, a comrade, and a soldier. Despite his absolute unbelievable physical abilities, he was discharged honorably before his thirty-six-month tour. This left him mentally and physically drained, and he grew even more withdrawn. His family knew something was wrong immediately and sought help for him, but he refused at first. His defiance was expected, but the family continued to slowly but surely support him and create avenues of employment that gave him better chances to select roads to recovery.

His family even paid for him to go to America where there were relatives Irving knew. They thought leaving Israel would be good for him, although they were, at times, despondent in their decision. As a result, he improved, but always, in the back of his mind, he longed for his military life with a free rein to kill and add misery to others who defied him.

Although Irving had been dropped from the Israeli army, he still had some people who thought he had been poorly treated and did not deserve his discharge. As it would be, he had kept in communication with some of them for several years after his release and while in the USA. He was contacted by one of them who had been approached secretly by some leaders of another country's Special Forces. They specifically needed a hard-nosed, well-trained, experienced and patriotic individual who could take charge of a new specialized unit of their special forces. They were looking for someone with a capacity to quickly prepare and execute complex, tactical, commando operations. His contact gave them his name, and soon he was in communication with the Argentinian Commando Company of their Special Operations Forces Group.

Irving spent some time preparing for this opportunity to regain his life of excitement, killing others, a place where he felt he belonged. Although he felt a bit rushed, he made reservations on Air USA Flight 2222.

~~ ~~ ~~

Helen's life has been pretty well laid out for you, but Helen had a secret, too. Sure, she was mean to her mother-in-law and her husband. What you don't know is Helen meant to be mean. She always knew

Maria was sick. It wasn't a surprise. She always felt she was an outcast even when dating Rick. In actuality, she was somewhat liked by his family at first, but her paranoia made her believe she was an outcast.

You see, Helen was bipolar, on medications, in therapy, and her doctors could never find the right dosages to keep her thoughts and actions under control. What they didn't understand was that she liked the fact that she had these ups and downs. They excited her beyond what anyone could imagine, and she never ever told anyone, medical professional or her family, how much of a thrill she had being out of control.

This was the reason why her medications wouldn't work. She purposely would not take them in order to obtain that overwhelming and indescribable sensation she got when off them. She hated the lows, but they were not as frequent as her highs. The insomnia, loss of energy and concentration were awful, but she was thankful they were not very often. Her highs were more euphoric with plenty of energy. Her impulsive sexual relationships led her to risky places and some despicable people. She had to learn to deal with them by elevating her mood to include combativeness and physical abuse.

Unlike others with bipolar disorder, she could control some of her actions, and she brought herself down using her medications. She was so adroit at hiding this ability, no one was ever aware of it, even her therapist or friends. When on her high, she harassed anyone, but Maria was her favorite target. It was as if she wanted her to become sick because of her, not her disease. She really was devilish to the point of evil and manipulated people so well, they thought her to be just a stronger, slightly overbearing woman.

During her treatment programs, she met other bipolar people and took those times to learn how they acted and what they did to make other people miserable. She incorporated these into her thoughts, modified them, and created ingenious ways to design her own schemes. For instance, being unaffected by poison ivy, she deliberately rubbed it over her breasts and between her legs before one of her sex sessions, just to torment her partner and enjoy his misery the next day. This was what she did for pleasure; however, she never admitted to herself that she was a purposely hateful human being. She always denied this and chalked it all up to her illness.

After her divorce, she wallowed in self-pity and couldn't wait for something in her life to occur so she could gloat over her mother-in-law and her family. Maria's death was just the moment. She let everyone know she was going to Argentina to reveal her 'remorse', hoping Rick's family would hear about it and be ready for her repentant arrival, but she wasn't going to do this at all. She was purposely going to stop her medications while there and become the best witch she could be and hopefully ruin the entire funeral and reception afterward. Revenge would be sweet for her, at last.

Hence, Helen was chosen to be a passenger on Air USA Flight 2222.

~~ ~~ ~~

Last, and certainly not least, is Frank Mason. He wasn't the total man portrayed in this story. Yes, everything about him, his life, his wife, and his profession are true, but his past was full of malignant behavior. He was obsessed with success. He longed for enormous achievements in everything he did, and he went to great lengths to get them. He was highly intelligent, for sure, but used it all to implement deceitful methods to get what he wanted. It made no difference how badly the lives he destroyed or the methods he used, just as long as his superiors never found out and those affected never knew he was their nemesis.

This was an acquired characteristic. He had done so as a child, a teenager, and a young adult in college. Whether it was being the elementary school's best in class, an officer of the student council, or the president of his college class, he manipulated people and pitted them one against another, causing argumentative meetings over the smallest of issues or clandestinely initiating fisticuffs between participants in club activities. He had devised some malicious plans to disrupt someone or groups of people from succeeding at something he felt would benefit his desired aim in life.

Even Kate had no idea of his purposeful improprieties. She was completely unaware of how deceitful he could be. There was a very good reason for this. He was never that way around her. He had succeeded in diverting his mean disposition from those who gave him comfort from his personal wretchedness. He found it difficult in the beginning, but as he grew up, it became easier and easier to the point when it had become second nature to him.

So, you can now see why he was the one chosen to go to Argentina for his company. He had succeeded in destroying his opposition—even if they were a better choice for the job—and pulled the wool over the eyes of the partners. By all accounts, Frank Mason spent his entire life as a fake.

It is on these grounds that Frank was the number one passenger conscripted to be on Air USA Flight 2222.

Afterword

One of the many morals of Rod Serling's *Twilight Zone* was always live a good life because if you don't or won't, you will end up regretting it and paying dearly for it. Nine characters, either through their past experiences or because they were left to their own devices earlier in life, have now found themselves forever regretting and paying for the deeds of their pasts.

The punishment, if you will, was chosen by all of the people whose lives they purposely destroyed. Those trashed desires and dreams have created the nine survivors' repetitive nightmare: the crash signifying the destruction of those lives; the raft as their chosen inner isolation in life; death as life's ultimate finality; sharks conveying hunger for power and fearmongering; cannibalism as a primitive, unabashed aggression; the paucity of drinking water representing the little goodness in their lives; the flying fish proclaiming a brief respite from the ravages of despair; the pirates decimating their heightened hopes; the interminable time on the ocean representing the infinite period they will spend in their common dream; and the ultimate rescue covertly initiating the same recurring nightmare.

Nine people lived a life of deceit, manipulation, physical and mental abuse, or revenge, and, as a result, have earned the dire consequence of Sisyphus but much more deeply devastating, as each one repetitively survives a vortex of misery and false hope within the same dream while traveling to Hell and back with eight equally wicked people.

Made in the USA
Middletown, DE
22 February 2022

61676924R00189